PAM'S GARDEN

M. LEE PRESCOTT

Pam's Garden
By M. Lee Prescott

Published by Mt. Hope Press
Copyright 2019, M. Lee Prescott

Cover Image Copyright: iStock/wundervisuals and Bigstock/jenyateua
ISBN: 978-1-7330217-4-6

AUTHOR WEBSITE
This book is a work of fiction. Names, characters, places, and events are products of the author's imagination or are used fictitiously. Any resemblance to actual people (alive or deceased), locales, or events is entirely coincidental.

For my sisters and the sisters of the Maple Tree Club

CHAPTER 1

"If you don't have your things out by noon, I'm calling the cops," Sandy Rodriguez said, glaring at the lanky blonde slouched at his kitchen counter.

A struggling artist, Becca had come to the club one night with friends and latched on to its handsome owner. Sandy had sworn off women after a string of unsuccessful relationships, but Becca had been witty, and she made him laugh. They'd gone out to dinner a couple of times, and she became a regular at Sandy's, the music venue he owned north of the village of Horseshoe Crab Cove. Then one day, he came home from work to find that she had moved all her stuff into his house. Too tired to deal with things that night, it was now a week later and he'd had enough.

Becca screwed her face into a pout. "Fine boyfriend you turned out to be."

"I'm not your boyfriend, Becca, and I never invited you to move in. Now, are you going, or do I—?"

"Fine!" She pushed back her stool, sloshing coffee onto the white marble counter. "You would call the cops too, wouldn't you?"

Damn straight, he thought, but said nothing, watching as she dragged the bags he'd placed in the front hall out to her car. Murphy, his club manager, had advised him to change the locks, and Sandy had scheduled the locksmith to arrive in an hour. No more hiding a key under the mat either. As he watched her sullen progression, he decided Becca Martin was not as pretty as he'd first thought. *Too pinched and scrawny. More like a swizzle stick than a woman.* Nothing like Pam Morgan, whom he'd seen around town a few times and taken out for one memorable how-are-you drink. Not that he was looking. *No more women for you, buddy.*

Becca plopped into her beat-up sedan and started the engine, never once looking back. As she drove out the driveway, she thrust her hand out, middle finger up. *Nice,* he thought, turning to go back into the house. Just as he was about to close the door, he spied a jogger coming up the street. Becca headed right for her, and the woman had to jump into a thick bush of rosa rugosa at the side of the road to avoid the car. Sandy ran down the steps to assist and was surprised to find the object of his recent daydreams, Pam Morgan, untangling herself from the thorny beach roses.

"Hi, Pam, sorry," he called. "Are you okay?"

"What's the matter with her?" Pam asked as she gazed up and recognized him. "Oh, it's you."

Sandy Rodriguez was well known to her family from the summer he'd worked for them in Maine when he was a teenager. Fifteen years younger than him, Pam had only vague recollections of their handsome summer employee who her ten-year-old sister, Ava, had swooned over, but she had certainly swooned the first time she saw him in Horseshoe Crab Cove. The epitome of a Latin lover, the thirty-nine-year-old club owner with his long, dark hair, coal-black eyes, and body to die for gave off the kind of smoldering heat that was hard to ignore. They'd had a drink a month earlier, but that was it. Divorced with a string of ex-girlfriends a mile long, Sandy Rodriguez had danger written all over him.

He reached out his hand, and she grabbed hold, stepping back onto the road. Even in her discombobulated state, she experienced a frisson of sensation at his strong, firm grip. Sensation that coursed through her body head to toe. As soon as she regained her balance, she let go, her breath escaping in a whoosh.

"I'm really sorry," he said. "My fault. I kind of pissed her off."

Pam smiled, a beautiful open smile that was reflected in her pale blue eyes. Dressed in running shorts and a singlet, she wore her long strawberry blonde hair tied back in a loose ponytail. *And oh, those legs!* He might have sworn off women, but he hadn't figured on half-naked Pam Morgan jogging down his street. Realizing he was gawking, he asked, "Do you live around here?"

"About a mile that way." She point down Beach Road. "I just moved into a rental. I love it."

"Oh, which house?" She paused for a second, and he added, "Sorry if that sounded nosey."

"No, more like neighborly," she said. "I'm in the Fergusons' right next to Frankie Brown."

"The hobbit house. Frankie's, I mean. She's one of my mom's good friends."

She smiled again, shielding her eyes from the bright sun. "They're both Darn Yarners, I believe?"

He laughed. "There aren't many people in this town who aren't connected to that group in some way. We're an incestuous bunch."

"You're lucky. Lucy, my stepmother, talks about how the Yarners saved her mom's life and how much they did for her and her sisters growing up."

"Ditto to that. Hey, can I offer you a drink? Water or something? Least I can do for almost getting you killed."

Pam hesitated, then said, "Well, a quick drink of water would be welcome, actually. It's hotter than I thought, and I didn't bring my water bottle."

"Great, come on up."

She followed him up the steps of a modern two-story house. The street side was plain with board-and-batten siding stained light gray, the front door moss green, but inside, it was light, airy, and warm, with soaring ceilings and glass everywhere.

Pam gazed agape. "Wow, this is a cool place. Did you build it?"

"More like restored or kind of leveled and rebuilt on the footprint. It's a work in progress. Come on back. We can sit on the deck. I'm expecting a contractor soon, so we may get interrupted." He led her through an ultramodern kitchen with light gray cabinets and beautiful white marble counter tops.

"These are unusual," she said, admiring the six stools that appeared to be made out of bleached driftwood.

"Tim Miller's designs. Told him what I wanted, and he built them, but then you'd know his work, wouldn't you?"

Pam nodded. "My sister's fiancé. He's incredibly talented, but I've never seen anything like this in his shop."

"That's one of the great things about Tim's work. He rarely repeats himself, so all his pieces are one of a kind." He pulled a pitcher from the fridge and poured water into two tall, frosted glasses. "He's a good buddy of mine. Here you go."

His fingers grazed hers as he handed her the glass. Pam was dismayed to feel her knees wobble. *Get a grip, girl!* she thought, following him out to the deck. "Wow, and I thought I was in heaven at the rental!" She gazed, open-mouthed, at his views of the river and bay beyond.

"Yeah, I'm lucky. This is why I bought the place."

As they chatted, gazing out at the river, Pam was aware of her body responding to every cadence of his rich, husky voice. *He's miles too old for you and a lothario to boot,* she thought as the doorbell chimed and he turned toward the house.

"That's my contractor. Excuse me?"

As he disappeared into the house, Pam came to her senses. Sandy Rodriguez was not only an older man and a playboy, he was also the ex-husband of Lolly LaSalle, her stepmother Lucy's business partner. It had been a very acrimonious divorce, supposedly due to his many infidelities. Lolly still referred to him as "the unmentionable." Gail, her sister, had dubbed him "poison" the one time Pam had remarked about how gorgeous he was. *Time to go, girl!*

Pam hopped up and went into the house. She placed her empty glass in the farmhouse-style stainless kitchen sink that had probably cost more than her week's salary as a social worker. Sandy was in the front hall chatting with the contractor, so she went through. "Mind if I use your bathroom before I head out?" she asked, nodding to the short, bald man with him.

"Sure, I'm in the middle of a renovation of the one down here, so head up the stairs, second door on the right."

She left them and climbed the stairs, passing what appeared to be a child's bedroom. Maisie's, she thought, Sandy's six-year-old-daughter with Lolly LaSalle. It was a light, open space, fuzzy rugs on the floors. A simple four-poster covered in a pastel patchwork quilt and lined with stuffed animals was painted a distressed white matching the dresser and side tables. Bookshelves lined one wall, holding dolls, games, puzzles, and a large collection of books. Lolly and Lucy owned Merlin's Closet, a children's book business, and Pam idly wondered how many of the collection had come from there.

Realizing she'd lingered too long, she hurried in and out of the bathroom also designed with a child in mind. Before heading downstairs, she tiptoed along the hall, peeking into another bedroom that appeared to be used for storage and then the master suite at the far end of the hall, its floor-to-ceiling windows offering spectacular water views. She wanted to go in and peek at his bathroom, which she imagined would be beyond impressive, but she heard his voice calling from below. "Find it okay?" Pam blushed, realizing she'd been caught snooping.

As she descended the stairs, she said, "I couldn't resist peeking into your daughter's room. It's beautiful. She must love it here."

"Not as much as her mom's house at present," he said, "but we keep workin' on it."

"I've got to get going," she said. "Thanks for the water."

"My pleasure. Feel free to use this as your pit stop anytime you see my truck in the yard." His smile took her breath away. *No wonder every woman in town is in love with him!*

"I'll remember that."

"Say hi to your dad for me."

"Will do," she said, slipping out before her legs turned to jelly. *One more minute staring into those eyes and who knows what might happen?*

As she headed out, Pam noticed the van in the drive, "Cove Locksmiths" on its side, and wondered if the reason for its presence was the wild woman who had almost run her over.

When she arrived back home, Gail was sitting on her front steps. "Where have you been?" When Pam explained, her sister shook her head. "What did I tell you about him—poison!"

Pam felt her cheeks redden. "It was a glass of water, not a proposition."

"From what I hear, everything's a proposition with Sandy Rodriguez!"

Probably right, Pam thought as they headed into the house.

CHAPTER 2

"Hey Murph," Sandy said, finding his manager in the kitchen of the club.

"Hey, boss, where you been?" Murph had been with him since he opened Sandy's ten years earlier. He knew his boss inside out, and they had become close friends. The tall redhead was built like a brick shithouse, which came in handy when he was pressed into service as the club bouncer.

"Following your advice and supervising the locksmith."

"So you managed to evict her?"

He related the incident with Becca and then went on to describe the encounter with Pam Morgan. Finally, he said, "Yup, and Peppy changed all the locks, so I'm good. I've hidden a spare key under the mermaid on the deck," he said, referring to a small cast-iron replica of the Little Mermaid statue in Copenhagen. He had commissioned Coop Merrick, the village blacksmith, to make it for Maisie, who loved the movie and Hans Christian Andersen story.

"Better hope the devious and cunning Ms. Martin doesn't find it."

"Geez, I hope not. I'm praying she's left town since her friends live up the coast."

Murph studied his boss for a minute. "Think you'll ever find anyone you stick with?"

"Nope."

"'Cause you're still in love with Lolly?"

Sandy gave him a look. "I love her, always will, but not in that way. She's the mother of my child, but beyond that common ground, we're not compatible, believe me."

"Well, you're not getting any younger, boss."

"You should talk. How long have you and Sasha been together now?" Ten years younger than his boss, Murph lived with a woman, Sasha Foster, to whom he claimed to be committed. Sandy liked Sasha, but he didn't see a long-term relationship there.

"Two years. We're a work in progress. When she finishes law school, we'll see. I'm guessing the Cove's not quite big enough for her."

"And you won't move with her?"

Murph grinned. "And give up my dream job? No fuckin' way, man."

Sandy laughed. "You're so full of shit, Murphy O'Neill. You know that, don't you?"

"So what about Pam Morgan? Sounds like you're interested."

"Nice kid. Too young, too normal. She was a toddler when I met her in Maine."

"Sounds like she's grown up now."

"Oh yeah, she's grown up, all right and she's gorgeous, but I know her dad. He'd kill me if I dicked her around."

"Hmm… That is a problem," Murph said. "Almost as serious as getting all the beer cooled for tonight. Gotta get cracking. Where is the rest of our lackadaisical staff?"

"Out enjoying this incredible day," Sandy said. "Come on, I'll help you." As he followed Murph into the storeroom, he thought about Pam Morgan's blue eyes and wondered just how angry Richard Morgan, her dad, would be if they dated and Sandy unintentionally broke his daughter's heart.

*****

"So… Tell me all about Mr. Poison," Gail said as they settled at the Crab Café for lunch.

"There's nothing to tell, and he's not Mr. Poison. He's actually a really nice guy."

"Not according to his ex."

Pam frowned at her sister. "How many people love their exes?"

"Lucy would have a fit if she knew you guys were dating."

"I barely know the man," Pam said. "We had one drink a month ago. Period. There's no dating on the horizon."

"Hmm… I would bet big money he'll make a move," Gail said, nodding as the waitress refilled their iced teas and placed their BLTs in front of them.

"Would you stop, please!"

Gail gave her a haughty look. "And what about Ava? She'd be devastated if you started dating her old beau."

"Our dear sister was ten when she had that ridiculous, and embarrassing, crush on him, and she is now *very* happily married."

"First loves last forever!" Gail sang, waving her hands.

"Change of subject, please. What's the latest with you and Heathcliff?" she asked, referring to Tim, Gail's fiancé. "Are you guys moving in together, or do you want to move in with me?"

"I'm staying put for the moment," Gail said. She and her sister, Weezie, lived with her dad, his new wife, Lucy, and her stepmother's two teenagers in the very large and beautiful farmhouse Richard Morgan had built on his farm and winery, Morgan's Fire.

They spent the remainder of the meal talking about the farm and all the projects happening with the wild horse rescue program, the progress of their few thoroughbreds and the winery at the farm's north end. Finally, Pam said, "Gosh that was a great sandwich. This place alone is worth the move from Maine. Want dessert?"

Gail set down her napkin. "Always, but I'll skip."

"Me too. Let's settle up. I want to show you something." Pam gestured to the waitress for the check.

The sisters strolled down Main Street until they reached the curve in the road that led to the north side of the peninsula. "Here we are," Pam said. They stood in front of Village Hardware.

Gail eyed her, puzzled. "This is what you want to show me? What? Have you convinced Dad to bankroll your purchase of the hardware store?"

"I wish. I love these kinds of places, which are, unfortunately, disappearing in the wake of Home Depot, Lowes, and Walmart. No, come on. She's around the back."

Pam led her around to a side door with a small sign that read "Bannister Landscaping."

She knocked, then opened the door, stepping into a large open space with several tables and all manner of garden equipment. The walls were lined with pegboard where hoes, rakes, shovels, pickaxes, and a number of tools, buckets, gloves, and hats hung. An earthy smell surrounded them as a bespectacled young woman rose from one of the tables and came to greet them.

"Welcome, ladies." The woman, clad in faded jeans and a Village Hardware T-shirt, had shoulder-length wispy blonde hair tied back in a sloppy ponytail and a pencil tucked behind her ear. Short and wraith thin, she exuded wiry strength in every fiber of her body.

"Gail, this is Kitty Bannister. Kitty, my sister, Gail."

The women shook hands as Gail gazed around. "Wow, this is a cool space. I didn't know you were back here."

"My secret warren. Uncle Tom set it up for me," Kitty said, grinning. Tom "Tack" Walsh owned Village Hardware. A widower, he and his wife, Ellen, had never had children so village gossip had it that they spoiled all their nieces and nephews. She turned to Pam. "I've got everything laid out. Want to take a look?"

The sisters followed her to one of the tables, where several blueprints lay. "Voilà!" Pam said, turning to Gail, then back to the table. "Oh, Kitty, these are beautiful. Just what I envisioned."

Kitty smiled. "Gonna be cool."

Gail gazed at the drawings, a puzzled look on her face. "What is this?"

"Plans for the healing and sensory garden I'm creating," Pam said. "It's been a dream of mine, and now Kitty and Dad are helping to make it a reality."

"At Morgan's Fire?" Gail said.

"No, with Dad's help, I convinced Mavis LaSalle to donate two acres of her property to the village. It's a five-minute walk from here. It's at the very edge of her land, and she was never going to use it. Now it's about to become a community garden. A special kind of community garden where kids and adults can come, have small plots, get their hands dirty. And it'll be handicapped accessible. The raised beds are extra high, which makes it much more accessible to older people who are more comfortable gardening in chairs or for kids in wheelchairs.

"The sensory idea came from that garden we saw in Sussex, remember?" Pam said, referring to their recent trip to England.

"I do," Gail said. "This is amazing."

"And, if all goes well, we break ground next month," Pam said.

They spent a while talking over the plans with Kitty, then the sisters walked the short distance to the garden site, an open field dotted with shrubs, small trees, and wildflowers. Pam sighed. "Isn't it beautiful?"

"Sure is," Gail said. "I can't believe you kept this a secret so long."

"I wanted to make sure it would happen. I wanted to tell you, but it's happened very fast, actually. Mavis signs the papers next week. It's been a dream of mine for so long. Plus it honors Mom." Even after two decades, Laura Morgan's children missed their loving mother, who had been an avid gardener.

Gail put her arm around her sister. "I'm proud of you, sis. Gonna be very cool. Of course you know what this means, don't you?"

Pam stared at her. "What?"

"It means that there's no way you can get involved with Mavis's ex-son-in-law. Mavis hates him."

"We not involved!" Pam said, even as her heart sank. *Gail is right. Any association with Sandy Rodriguez might be the kiss of death for the garden.*

"Well, keep it that way," Gail said. "Let's walk back, and I'll buy you an ice cream cone to celebrate!"

CHAPTER 3

"I'm proud of you, Pammie," Richard Morgan said as the family enjoyed Sunday dinner together seated at the enormous farm table Richard had commissioned from Tim Miller. It replaced the one they'd brought from Maine, and it seated twenty-five. Today, there were nineteen diners, including Tim Miller, Gail's fiancé, and Lucy's sister Harriet, and Kyle Morgan, her fiancé, as well as Helen Winthrop, Lucy and Harriet's mom.

Since Lucy and her teenagers Amy and Rob moved to the farm, the extended family made it a point to share Sunday dinner. Most weeks, Teddy made the trip from Providence, and occasionally, Ben Morgan drove up from Philadelphia. Depending upon the week, there could be fourteen to twenty-something diners around the huge farm table. Gus Casey, the farm manager and head horse trainer, was always welcome with his family, but they usually spent Sundays in Connecticut with his wife Lynn's family.

"Thanks, Dad," Pam said. "It's gonna be cool. Kitty's incredibly talented. She's designed a garden that even Mavis will love."

"Would there be a place for my arbor?" Lucy asked. "No pressure, but I commissioned it from Coop Merrick before your dad and I got serious, and I didn't want to leave it at the old house."

"Are you sure?" Pam asked. "It's so beautiful. Wouldn't you guys like to find a spot for it here?"

Her father shook his head. "It's yours. Coop delivered it last week. It's in the barn ready to go. If we want an arbor someday, we'll commission another one."

Pam exchanged a look with Gail, then said, "Thank you so much, Lucy. It will provide a lovely entry to the gardens."

"I'd love to help, if you need workers," Lucy's daughter Amy said, her eyes never straying far from Wolfie, Pam's brother. Amy adored Wolfie.

"That'd be terrific," Pam said. "We should be ready to start building the beds next weekend." Along with her brothers and sisters, Pam had assembled a crew of townspeople to construct the bed boxes and haul dirt.

Wolfie grinned. "We'll make short work of it, sis. Even Zeke claims he's coming and Cara, too." He referred to his coworkers at the vineyard, resident vintner Zeke Ravenstock and Cara Feldspar, his assistant, who had just recently moved into their new homes on the Morgan's Fire vineyard property.

"Speaking of Zeke," Gail said. "Has everyone checked out the vineyard website this week? It's finally up and running and features profiles of Zeke, Cara, and our devilishly handsome manager, Jonathan 'Wolfie' Morgan."

Ava turned to Wolfie. "Aw, you chickened out and went with Jonathan? What fun is that?"

Wolfie grinned. "You already need a microscope to read my résumé, so we didn't want to scare people off with Wolfie. Might put them in mind of werewolves."

"Since you look like one!" Weezie said, jabbing him.

"Jonathan's classy," Gail said. "I like it, and it's a great shot of him."

"Yes, it is," Lucy said. "Very distinguished and handsome."

The youngest Morgan, Wolfie had long dark hair, a thick beard, and piercing coal-black eyes. He was born shortly before his mother's death. During her pregnancy, Laura Morgan had refused treatment for the cancer that had spread through her body. She chose to save her son instead of endure treatments that might have saved her life but harmed her unborn child. Despite his father's reassurances over the years, Wolfie carried that burden and was old beyond his twenty-two years.

Wolfie had taken the year off from a five-year physical therapy program, then switched gears and completed an online business and management degree from Wharton. Until he accepted the job as manager of Morgan's Fire Winery, he'd been working part-time at Merlin's Closet, Lucy and Lolly's children's book business.

The photo in question was taken near the edge of the restored vineyard, and behind the young, gorgeous entrepreneur lay acres of grapevines as far as the eye could see. Wolfie, in an open-collared blue shirt, wind in his hair, looked every bit the part of a robust, successful vintner. Presently he was on a crash course to learn the wine business so he could live up to the PR campaign. To this end, he would depart in the morning for an extended tour of wineries all over the country.

"Wish I was going with you," Richard said. "Maybe I'll fly out when you're in the Valley visiting the Dillons."

"I'm in!" Weezie said.

"I'm only in the Valley for two days," Wolfie said. "And it's work."

Pam watched the interplay between brother and sister and decided a change of subject was in order. "So you two," she said, looking down the table at Gail and Tim. "Have you decided on a date?"

"We're thinking June twelfth," Gail said.

"Yikes that's only three weeks away!" Weezie said.

"It's actually four," Gail said, "and remember, we're doing small and simple."

Her father threw up his hands. "How can you do small and simple with the Miller clan and all us Morgans?"

"Simple and low-key might be more accurate," Tim said.

Gail nodded. "Yes, simple…simple…simple. Tim's family wants to have a party the night before and we want to be married here at the farm, in the barn, if that's okay?"

"Okay, we'd love it, princess," Richard said. "But can we pull things together that fast?"

"You bought all the tables and chairs for your wedding, so all we need is tablecloths. Salters will do the rest. They've saved the date for the reception. We want to do a clambake."

"In a bridal gown?" Weezie said.

"I'm wearing a simple dress that I love and that I can wear again," Gail said. "I picked it out last week. After the ceremony, I'm changing into jeans."

"Where'd you get the dress?" Pam asked.

Gail smiled. "Vintage Threads in Bayport."

"Uh-oh," Weezie said.

"Hush," Pam said, poking her youngest sister. "It's Gail and Tim's wedding."

"Sounds like lots of fun," Lucy said. "Please let us know what we can do."

They spent the rest of the meal talking about the wedding preparations and numbers. Richard said he wouldn't be surprised if some of the Valley family might return even though they'd been here only a month earlier for his and Lucy's wedding. Tim had work to do, so he excused himself after dessert. As people dispersed or departed, the sisters decided to take a walk. Dan took the kids home, so Ava, Gail, Weezie, and Pam headed out. Wolfie walked with them as far as the trail that led north to the vineyard. The four women decided to walk part of the Loop Trail toward the village.

"So talk about a bombshell," Ava said as they waved goodbye to their brother. "You're a woman of hidden depths, Gail Morgan."

"It's just sort of come together. We didn't want to wait. It always seems like someone's getting married, and we decided to jump the queue and do it. We want to find a place together too. Actually, much as I love them, I wouldn't be entirely disappointed if the western crew stayed back. We'll be seeing them next winter, and it's such a lot of orchestration to find places for them all."

"There's always the Bayport Inn," Ava said. "It's pretty nice. That's where they put people when they come for meetings at the Lab." Ava and her husband, Dan, worked at a research lab on the waterfront in town.

"Take it off your plate," Pam said. "One of us will phone them and block off rooms. We can also check with Mavis."

Gail shook her head. "She's booked solid from now till October, all the cottages and the rooms in the house. That's what I mean about orchestration."

"We'll figure it out," Pam said. "Maybe we could even beg rooms at Harriet's school. I'll bet the boarders have gone home for summer by then."

"That's an idea," Gail said. "Thanks, ladies. Now, let's enjoy the view. I refuse to let the entire month be swallowed up with wedding planning. Faith Miller's got her army working over there for the Friday night party so thankfully, we have no part of that. Just have to give her numbers."

Pam's phone buzzed, and she pulled from her pocket to spy a text from her colleague. She had begun working as a part-time school social worker and counselor the past month and was already heavily into school activities. She and Greta Jeffers, her fellow counselor, had volunteered to assist with a community fundraiser, and suddenly, they'd found themselves in charge. Committees had been working on raffle and auction items for months before they became involved. The event was in two weeks, and the venue they'd booked had a fire and had cancelled on them. Greta had been searching for an alternative. The text read: *Great news. Sandy's has agreed to host, so it's full speed ahead.*

"Interesting," Pam said, slipping the phone back in her pocket. "Sisters, remember the fundraiser I roped you into buying tickets for? Well, since the fire at the Lagoon, we've been scrambling to find an alternate venue. It's now gonna be at Sandy's, so lace up your dancing shoes!"

CHAPTER 4

Sandy looked over the counter at his five-year-old daughter. She had devoured four slices of pizza and was now halfway through a bowl of rainbow vanilla ice cream. "You sure you don't want to stay over sweet pea? I can take you to school tomorrow."

Maisie shook her head. "Mommy's comin' for me."

"But we could ask her."

"She'll say no. 'Sides, I gotta help Nana."

"Help Nana do what?"

"She's got a lot of functions."

"And a team of workers. What does she have you doing?"

"Favors. I scoop the candies into the bags. Nana says I'm the best."

"I'll just bet she does. Want more, baby?"

Ignoring him, Maisie gazed out the window. "There's Mommy!" she cried, hopping down from the stool.

"Maisie, wait. She'll come in," he called, but she'd already thrown open the door and was running to meet her mother in the drive.

Lolly looked up as he appeared in the doorway. "Hey, is she all set?"

"Technically, this is still my time."

"I know, but it's a school night. Sweetie, run up and get your things. Don't forget Snickers," she said, referring to Maisie's favorite stuffed animal, a well-loved teddy bear, a gift from her father.

"Snickers is in the den, baby," he called. "Want to come in for a sec? I guarantee her stuff's scattered all over the place."

Lolly hesitated, then walked toward him. "Just for a minute. We've got to get back. Mom needs us."

"I wish you wouldn't make plans for her Sunday nights, Loll. This is *my* time and really the only time I can reliably count on being free."

Lolly shrugged, stepping into his front hallway. "Not my fault. You have a slew of employees. Can't they take over so you have more free time?" She gazed around. "Boy, this place is really coming along, isn't it?"

"Maisie told me she has to get back to help Nana. What's that all about?"

"She loves helping with wedding prep."

"Wouldn't you get a lot more done if she stayed with me?"

"Maybe." Lolly continued to wander through rooms, an occasional eyebrow raised as she surveyed their surroundings. "Sandy's must be doing *really* well for you to afford all this."

"I don't want to fight about this, Loll, but it seems as if you always have some important thing planned for Sunday night so Maisie doesn't want to stay."

"Don't be ridiculous. Mom's business is twenty-four seven, you know that."

"If you guys didn't insist she was indispensable, she'd want to stay. I see little enough of her as it is."

"Now you're being paranoid. You're the big shot club owner who never has any time for his daughter."

"Bullshit."

Lolly threw up her hands. "Okay, okay, I'm not doing this. Maisie, where are you, baby?"

Conversations with Lolly usually followed this pattern. He'd try to be reasonable, Lolly would stonewall, then finally accuse. If he'd heard it once, he'd heard it a thousand times how he never had time for his daughter. "I can easily make time. Just tell me the days and I can arrange it with Murph."

"You say that, and the next thing I know, Maisie's hanging out with you and the guys at the club."

"At least we don't break any child labor laws like you and your mom."

"Don't be ridiculous. Maisie, come on!"

"All I'm asking is that we collaborate on true joint custody. Not a half day here and there."

Maisie appeared at the head of the stairs, a bulging backpack on one arm, Snickers on the other. "Ready!"

Sandy held out his arms, and she ran down into them. "Bye, Daddy."

"See you soon, baby." He ruffled her blonde curls, then set her down. "Be good and have fun at school."

Lolly took the backpack. "You head out, precious. I'll be right there." She turned to him. "We can talk more. Promise."

"Thanks," he said, knowing full well nothing would happen. Lolly's anger lurked just below the surface, anger at him for the hurt. He didn't blame her, but he wished they could somehow move on. "Have a good week."

"You too," she said, slipping into the car.

Sandy checked the straps of Maisie's car seat, gave her one more kiss, and shut the door.

"See you later, alligator!" Maisie sang.

"Afternoon, baboon," he replied, grinning as Lolly backed out of the drive.

In the growing darkness, he waved as Lolly's car disappeared. A gray Subaru came down the street and stopped next to his driveway. Pam Morgan waved. "Hi, neighbor!"

"Hey," he said, coming to greet her. "What brings you to this neck of the woods?"

"I just dropped my sister Ava off, and I'm headed home."

"How 'bout a nightcap?"

Pam hesitated, then said, "Why not. But I can't stay long. It's a school night."

"Where have I heard that before?"

"Excuse me?"

He smiled, that killer smile as he opened the door for her. "Ignore me. I heard something about you working at the school."

"Yes, I am. And speaking of that, thank you so much for hosting the school fundraiser at Sandy's. We were desperate."

"You're involved in that?" he asked, noticing the delicious curve of her ass as she preceded him up to the house.

"My colleague Greta and I volunteered to help. The original co-chairs quit, and suddenly, we're running the thing. Fortunately, they'd already done most of the work."

Sandy closed the front door, facing her, their bodies almost touching. "Well then, we'll be working very closely together."

Pam felt her face redden, and she stepped back. "Something like that."

Sandy grinned, coal-black eyes sparkling with mischief. "So what'll you have?"

Flustered, she stammered, "Excuse me?"

"To drink? Nightcap? I have just about everything. Just name it. I also have an excellent brandy."

"Truthfully, I'm not much of an aperitif person. Whatever you're having, I'll have a tiny glass of the same."

He gestured toward the living room. "Make yourself at home. The deck's my favorite place at this time of night. We have about forty-five minutes before the mosquitos take over."

Rooted to her spot, Pam stood watching him, wondering if she should bolt now before she did something foolish. He grabbed two snifters from the bar and poured a half inch of brandy in each, then handed one to her. "Come on. Outside okay?" He placed his hand on the small of her back.

As fire coursed through her, she was amazed to feel her legs moving. "Fine," she said as they stepped out into the cool of the evening.

He sat on an upholstered swing and patted the seat beside him. "Best seat in the house."

Pam sat at the end, as far from him as possible.

Sandy watched her, grinning. "I don't bite, you know."

"Yes, but you do have a bit of a reputation."

He shrugged. "Can't help that, I guess."

"So this is just a friendly nightcap?"

"Yup." Wolfish grin.

"Really?"

"Honestly? I find you very attractive."

"And? Is there a but there somewhere?" she asked.

"You tell me. I'd love to take this further, tonight or anytime, but this is a small town, and you're connected to people who hate my guts."

Pam took a gulp of liquid fire and sat up, staring at him. "I don't know anyone who hates your guts, and my dad loves you."

"Well, there's your new stepmother, for one. Anyone associated with my ex is not gonna be one of my fans."

"That's silly," Pam said. "What people think or don't think doesn't matter one bit."

"Agreed."

"But what does matter is you're you and I'm me."

"Better explain that."

"You're a mature, experienced man who changes girlfriends every five minutes. In fact, they probably change so often, they don't even get to 'girlfriend' status, from what I hear."

"Whoa," he said, placing his brandy on the table. "You don't pull any punches, do you?"

"The other half of this equation is me. I'm relatively inexperienced and a one-man woman on the few occasions when I've even had a boyfriend. I would be way out of my depth with you."

"How do you know till you dive in?"

"I just know," she said.

"You are kind of naïve, like a deer in the headlights. But I find that really sexy."

Pam flushed from the brandy and the increasingly unsettling conversation. "See, that's what I mean! I've got to get going."

"You haven't finished your brandy."

Pam gulped the rest, her throat burning, body heated to boiling as she stood. "There, now I have." She hurried into the kitchen, set the snifter on the counter, and turned to find him a few feet behind her. "Thanks for the nightcap."

"Can we do it again?" he said.

"Probably not." Pam headed for the front door only to find it locked. As she struggled to unlatch it, he came up behind her, their bodies touching as he said, "Here, let me."

He unlatched the door and opened it, lips grazing her cheek as she slid out. "Great to see you, neighbor!" he called as she ran to her car.

Pam hopped in, exhaling an audible sigh as she turned the ignition. *Oh my goodness, that was close!* she thought as she drove away, afraid to look back.

Sandy watched her go. *Chances of getting to square one with Pam Morgan are slim to none, but boy, is she worth a shot!*

CHAPTER 5

"Hey, gal, where's the fire?" Greta Jeffers shouted as Pam flew by the guidance office Monday morning.

"Trouble in gym class. They just called," Pam called over her shoulder.

When she arrived, the class of ninth graders sat on the bleachers, the teacher at the far end of the room with two boys, Jared Cochran, morbidly obese and red as a beet, and Mickey Parks, a short, thin bully well known to Pam after six weeks of part-time work at the school. "How can I help?" she asked, addressing Pete Sanders, the gym teacher.

He explained that Mickey had shoved Jared, who fell flat on the floor and came up swinging. Pam took one look at Jared's eyes and the fury reflected in their brown depths and pulled out her cell phone, dialing the front office. She knew with certainty, as did Pete Sanders, that the situation was far from over. She stepped a few feet away and spoke to one of the secretaries, asking that the principal and the school safety officer join them immediately. As she turned back, wondering why they hadn't been called in the first place, Mickey said something under his breath, and Jared lunged at him, arms outstretched.

Before she knew what was happening, a fist hit her cheek, knocking Pam to the floor. Beside her, Jared had his hands around the smaller boy's neck, and Pete Sanders stood over them, trying to pull Jared off. Two other boys stepped in to assist, and between them, they separated Jared and Mickey. All three held Jared as Mickey coughed, holding his neck. Stunned, Pam tried to sit up and saw stars. Another student she didn't know came forward and crouched beside her. "You okay, Ms. Morgan?"

Pam gazed up at the petite redhead. "To be honest, I'm not sure." She reached up to touch her head and felt wetness. There was blood on her hand when she brought it down.

"Cathy," Pete Sanders called. "Run down and get the nurse. Hurry!"

The next few minutes were a blur as the principal and police officer arrived and escorted both boys out. Greta arrived along with the school nurse, Mary Souza, a short, dark-haired woman in colorful patterned scrubs. Together, they assisted Pam to the bleachers where she sat down, still dazed.

Mary flashed a light in her eyes. "Did you get knocked out?"

"I don't think so," Pam said.

"You may have a slight concussion. That's also a nasty gash that probably needs stitches. I'd suggest that you be seen by someone. Who's your primary?"

Pam shook her head. "I just moved, so I don't have a doctor yet."

"Dr. Brennan in Horseshoe Crab Cove is the school's on-call doc. Shall I call him?"

"Yes," Greta said. "I'll take her over."

"I'm not sure that's necessary," Pam said.

"Well, we are," Greta said. "Come on, girl."

On the drive, her head began to clear and Pam felt much better. "This is silly. I'm fine."

Greta patted her knee. "Better safe than sorry. Besides, Dr. Brennan's a hunk."

"And also my stepmother's ex, so I won't be signing up to be his patient."

"What does that matter?"

As they neared the outskirts of Horseshoe Crab Cove, Pam said, "This town's small enough already. Ooh, do I have a headache. Yikes, that Jared packs a mean wallop."

"They're going have to deal with that situation," Greta said. "It's not safe, and Mickey's not going to stop. Suspending him is absolutely no deterrent."

"Is that what happened?" Pam asked as Greta parked in the small lot behind Cove Medical Building.

"Who knows? I'm just guessing."

As it turned out, Dr. Brennan was doing hospital rounds, so Pam saw his associate, Cynthia Vogt, a slight woman with shoulder-length light brown hair, blue eyes and glasses. After taking her vitals and examining her, Dr. Vogt said, "You may have a slight concussion, your cheek's going to swell and be black and blue, and that gash needs a stitch or two. How did all this happen?"

"A wild punch knocked me over, and I must have hit the floor. Somehow, I guess I didn't have time to break the fall. Must've smacked down on the side of my head."

"Ordinarily, I'd send you to a plastic surgeon because the cut's on your face, but it's right at your hairline. I can do the stitches, unless you'd prefer the referral?"

"Can I look in a mirror?" Pam asked.

"Of course. Let me get one and an ice pack. Be right back."

"What a mess," Pam said as the doctor closed the door. "Just what I need. I'm sorry to pull you away too."

"No prob. This is my slow day."

"So what's new?" Pam asked, regarding her colleague and friend. Greta had a sharp, delicate beauty, oval face, violet eyes, and short-cropped hair. She was dressed in gray twill slacks and a deep-purple sweater that flattered her thin, waiflike figure. Pam knew her to be strong and athletic, but sometimes Greta looked like a strong breeze would blow her away.

"Not much, although I'm relieved we have our venue for the Spring Fling, which has been dumped solidly in our laps. I still can't believe it. I've recruited a few workers, but we need many more volunteers."

"I can rope in my siblings. They've kind of already volunteered."

"Great, well, that's a small army, then. We're going to have to go out to Sandy's and scope out the place. I was actually going to suggest that when you ran by me this morning. Maybe we can wait a day or two till you feel better?"

"I'm fine," Pam said. "Let's see what Dr. Vogt says."

The doctor stepped in with her nurse and a tray of equipment. She handed Pam a small hand mirror.

Pam studied the wound that followed the hair near her right temple. "Let's do it. I'm fine with you stitching that."

On the way back to school, ice pack on her swollen cheek and a small bandage covering her stitches, Pam said, "Since Dr. Vogt okayed me to drive, I think I'll take advantage and go home for the rest of the day."

Greta nodded. "Good plan."

"But I'm happy to drive up to Sandy's later. After we look things over, we can stop for supper at Baggy Wrinkle. I love their salads."

"Are you sure?" Greta asked as they pulled into the high school lot.

"Yes, of course. If you could give them a call and see if they'll be open? Sandy's, I mean?"

"Will do," Greta said as the two colleagues strolled into the building. Pam headed for the office to check in and let them know she was leaving.

As she headed to her car moments later, she thought, *What was I thinking? Happy to go to Sandy's indeed! I was so unnerved by the man, I practically sprinted out of his house last night, and now I have to face him looking like a prizefighter!*

CHAPTER 6

"Hey, boss," Murph called as Sandy carried boxes to the store room. "Just got a call from one of the fundraiser women, Greta something. They want to stop by later. You gonna be here?"

Sandy paused, resting a heavy box on the edge if the bar. "I can. Who's coming?"

Murph gave him a look, wondering at the question, then said, "I guess the woman who called and someone else maybe? She didn't say."

"What time?"

"Around five, five thirty. I've gotta make a run into town, but I'll be back by then if you're busy?"

"Naw, I'll be fine," Sandy said, wondering if Pam Morgan might be the someone else.

"You got a special interest in this project?" Murph asked, watching his boss with his eagle eye.

"Civic duty, man. Always interested in doing my part."

Murph gave him a look, but said nothing.

*****

Richard Morgan took one look at his daughter and said, "That's it! Time for you to quit and come work here."

Head pounding, Pam sat down at the dining room table, where her father and Lucy were finishing lunch. "I'm fine, Dad. Really. I like my work."

He shook his head. "Pay you nothing, hazardous conditions, what's the upside? Suppose one of those kids had had a gun? What then? Or 'spose one of them comes back with one next week?"

"This is the world we live in," Pam said, nodding to their housekeeper, Callie, who brought her a fresh ice pack.

"How frightening for you nonetheless," her stepmother said. "What will happen to the boys?"

Pam shook her head. "I don't know. I feel for Jared and his poor parents. They've tried everything."

Lucy nodded. "They're nice people. They run Cove Toys and Games. Have you been there?"

"Not yet. I'm guilty of ordering almost everything online," Pam said.

"Aren't we all? They have a small book section, mostly children's books, and they order regularly from us. We're always praying they don't go out of business. Anyway, I know they worry about Jared, poor thing."

"It's a shame they allowed him to get so huge, even though that doesn't excuse the bullying, of course," Pam said.

"Apparently, he spends a lot of time with his grandparents, who stuff the kids. Carol, his mom, has tried to curb it, but with the shop and her husband's other business, the grandparents are the primary caregivers."

"I empathize with your friends," Richard said, "but I'm thinking of my baby now."

Pam frowned, pain shooting through her cheekbone. "Dad, I am not your baby, and I love my job. I should have been more aware of the situation. I also should have called the safety officer to go down with me."

"Geez, what happened to you?" Gail said, joining them. She set a glass of iced tea and an egg salad sandwich on the table.

"That looks good," Pam said, wondering if it would hurt to chew.

Callie popped her head around the corner. "I can make you one."

Pam gave the housekeeper a crooked smile. "That would be great. Thanks, Cal."

"So? What happened?" Gail said.

Pam related the day's events, ending with, "And I met the doc I'd love for my primary. Do you know her? Cynthia Vogt?"

"She's in the same practice as my doc, Chuck Beaman," Richard said, stopping there rather than mentioning their associate, Rob Brennan.

"She's great," Lucy said. "If it wasn't awkward with Rob, I'd go to her. I really prefer a woman primary."

"Me too," Pam said.

"Where do you go?" Gail asked.

"I go to an all-women's practice in Northport," Lucy said. "My doc is Cara Summers."

As they discussed the relative merits of their various physicians, Richard said, "This is an unexpected pleasure to have both Lucy and Pam home for lunch. What's everyone's plan for the rest of the day?"

"I'm swamped with work and then I'm having dinner with Tim," Gail said.

"And I'm headed back to work in a bit," Lucy said. "Wish I could stay, but we're buried in new orders."

"I'm going to take a rest, then Greta and I are heading up to Sandy's, then out to dinner."

"Sandy's?" Gail gave her a sharp look.

Pam gazed from her sister to Lucy before saying, "They've come to the rescue for the school fundraiser after the Lagoon cancelled on us."

Lucy shook her head. "That was too bad about the fire. I hope they're planning to rebuild. Even though the food's marginal and the décor garish, the Lagoon's kind of an institution around here."

"So don't count on me for dinner," Pam said.

"Are you sure you should go anywhere today?" Gail frowned.

"I'm fine." Pam hurried out of the room to forestall any further interrogation.

CHAPTER 7

"Gosh, what a spot," Greta said as the two women got out of her jeep in front of Sandy's.

Pam nodded. "It does look pretty cool."

"Living in Southport, we tend to go to the Foc'sle. Can't believe I've never seen this place."

"Me either," Pam said, wishing she were a million miles away. "This is probably a mistake."

"Why? It's going to be perfect! And it's free." Greta fumbled with her purse, finally extracting it from the back seat before gazing over at Pam. "What's wrong?"

"I must look like a fright. Maybe I should wait in the car?"

Greta made a show of studying her for a few seconds. "You look great. Your hair covers the stitches, and your cheek isn't nearly as swollen. Besides, who cares? These guys don't, that's for sure. Probably some lackey will show us around."

"I'm sure you're right. Let's go." Pam stood straight and marched toward the main door of the club.

The door was locked, so they knocked. When no one came, Pam said, "Let's try around back."

Just as Pam turned away, the doors swung open. "Hey, welcome, ladies!"

Pam spied her friend's expression before she turned to face Sandy Rodriguez. For a second, she thought Greta might swoon. Pam turned to face the man from whom she had fled the previous evening, and her knees wobbled. His eyes registered concern. "Come on back. Sandy Rodriguez," he said, extending his hand to Greta. "And you are?"

"Oh my goodness, where are my manners?" Pam sputtered. "This is my colleague, Greta Jeffers. We're co-chairing the fundraiser."

"Delighted, Ms. Jeffers," he said, standing aside to let her pass.

"The pleasure is all ours, Mr. Rodriguez."

"Sandy, please. I'm old enough without sounding like my grandpa. Hey, Pam, how're you doing?" He leaned in, embracing her, a chaste kiss on her uninjured cheek.

Pam blushed crimson as she followed Greta inside.

"So you guys know each other?" Greta said. "Pam didn't say."

Sandy grinned. "We're kind of neighbors."

"Lucky Pam!"

This was a side of her colleague that Pam had never seen. Batting eyelashes, coy expressions. Greta hung on his every word as Sandy led them through the cavernous space to one of the bars. "So this is basically it. If it's a good night, you can use the decks too. What did you have in mind?"

Pam sat on the stool farthest from him, deciding she needed to take control of the situation. "Well, it's a dinner, then auction. We'll set up tables around the perimeter for the silent auction and items. We're considering hiring a band for dancing too."

"Well, you've come to the right place for that, except we don't do food beyond tapas and snacks."

"No prob," Greta said. "Salters is catering."

"A clambake?" He gazed from one to the other, his eyes lingering on Pam.

"No, barbecue," Greta said. "Simple, straightforward. They'll need to set up grills. Is there a good spot for that?"

Sandy reached around and pushed a button behind the bar. Almost immediately, the double doors at the other end of the room banged open, and a mini

Arnold Schwarzenegger stepped out. Red hair, blue eyes that sparkled even from across the room. "Yeah, boss?" He wore a black Sandy's T-shirt, the fabric stretched thin across his broad chest.

"Come meet the fundraising chairs. Pam Morgan, Greta Jeffers, this is my manager, Murphy O'Neill."

"Hey, ladies, it's Murph. Pleased to meet you."

"Not as pleased as we are," Greta said, rushing forward to shake his hand. "You guys are so incredibly generous to be doing this for us."

Murph smiled. "Don't look at me. I just work here. This was the boss's call."

"Oh, we know. Sandy's been phenomenal." More eyelash batting and silly grinning as Greta ping-ponged back and forth between the two men.

"Hey, Murph. Why don't you show Greta around out back. You guys can figure out about placement of the grills. We'll map out the interior space."

"Sure thing," Murph said.

When the others disappeared, he turned to Pam. "What the hell happened to you?"

"It's nothing. Have you got some paper for this mapping project."

"I'm serious, Pam," he said, placing a hand on her arm. "I'm concerned. You sure as hell didn't look like that yesterday."

"There was an altercation at school this morning. No big deal. I wasn't paying attention and got caught in the crossfire."

"That was some crossfire. Are you okay?"

Flustered at his attention and nearness, she sputtered, "Yes, thanks. Now can we?"

In answer, he stepped around the bar and returned with a legal pad and pencils. As they sketched a rough outline of the floor plan and discussed a number of details, Pam kept her distance, afraid he might touch her again. This could send her right off the deep end! Lady Gaga's lyrics, *I'm far from the shallow now*, echoed in her mind.

They'd been talking for a good fifteen minutes with no sign of the others. "Where do you think they are?" she asked.

"Maybe Murph took her for a beach stroll. It's pretty at this time of day. Hey, before they return, I want to say something about yesterday."

Pam put her hands up. "There's no need, really. Can we just forget about yesterday?"

"But I feel like I scared you off, and I wanted to apologize."

"No need. It was my overreaction."

His dark eyes held hers, mesmerizing, beautiful pools of inky light. "Could we start again? I'd love to have dinner some night."

"I don't think that's a good idea," she said, continuing to hold his gaze even as she began to tremble. *He is absolutely perfect, and he knows it.*

"It's just dinner, Pam."

"Here come the others," she said, hopping up from her stool.

"Can I call you?" he whispered.

Despite the warning bells clanging in her head, Pam gave him a slight nod.

"Great!" He turned to the others before she could change her mind. "Hey, guys, got everything worked out?"

"Sure do!" Greta said. "I wish you guys were free. You could join us at Baggy Wrinkle for dinner."

"As it so happens, we are," Sandy replied. "Or at least I am. Club's closed on Mondays."

"Me too," Murph said, grinning from ear to ear.

"Then it's settled," Greta said, ignoring Pam's frown. "Meet you there?"

CHAPTER 8

"What were you thinking?" Pam asked as they drove the short distance to Baggy Wrinkle Bistro.

"I was thinking we're single and those are two hot guys."

"Who may not even be single."

Greta shrugged. "Who cares? I didn't see any wedding bands."

"Well, I happen to know that Murph has a steady girlfriend."

"I thought you'd never met him?" Greta said. "Sandy either."

"I have met Sandy, but not Murph. But Murph's girlfriend, Sasha, is one of the instructors at the yoga studio in town that's owned by Tim's aunt."

"Tim?"

"Miller, soon to be my brother-in-law. Anyway, Sasha works with my brother Rich's erstwhile girlfriend, Sara, who's also a yoga teacher. I've taken a couple of classes from both women and I've heard them talk about boyfriends and your Murph in particular. I believe Sasha is angling for a commitment from him."

"So there you go—he's still on the market, and his gorgeous boss is—"

"Referred to as poison in my family. He's a wicked philanderer. Has a new woman on his arm every week."

"Sounds like he'd be a great time, even if short-lived. I got the feeling he was more interested in you than me, though," Greta said, feigning dejection.

"He couldn't be less interested in me!" Pam said.

Greta laughed, steering the jeep into Baggy Wrinkle's clamshell-covered parking lot. "Keep telling yourself that, dearie!"

Sandy's truck pulled in right behind them, and the couples met at the door. They had just been told there was an hour wait when the owner passed by and spied Sandy. "Hey, buddy. You eating?"

"In an hour, we hear," Sandy said, throwing up his hands.

Oliver Silva shook his head. "No way, Jose. How many of you?"

Sandy held up four fingers.

"Patty, give these guys my table. Pronto."

The tall, slender, strawberry blonde Patty in blue jeans and white Baggy Wrinkle shirt grabbed four menus and waved for them to follow. When they arrived at the table in a windowed alcove overlooking the water in three directions, Patty whispered, "Aren't you the lucky ones. He was saving this for family members tonight. There'll be hell to pay when they arrive."

Sandy slipped her some cash. "Why don't you put my name in for another table. Then if you have to bump us, we'll have somewhere to go."

Patty gave him a wink as she slid the cash into her pocket. *They've clearly done this dance before,* Pam thought, watching the inveterate flirt in action.

"This is spectacular," Greta said, sliding in next to Murph.

For someone with a steady girlfriend, Murphy O'Neill is treading on dangerous ground, Pam thought, watching the couple across the table. She was already furious at Greta for suggesting this and now for arranging the seating so she was inches away from Sandy Rodriguez on the cushioned, cozy window seat.

"You must come here often," Pam said, half turning toward him.

"Oliver's a friend. We went through school together," he replied.

"Of course he is," Greta said. "Everyone's friends with everyone around here except me. I'm a newcomer and always will be."

"Where're you from?" Murph asked.

"I grew up in Rhode Island. Barrington, mostly."

"Nice town."

"It was, but I wanted the big city. So look where I end up? Hicksville."

"Wouldn't live anywhere else," Sandy said.

"Yeah, but you had ten years in the big city," Murph said as the waitress came to take their orders.

"Hey, folks, your drinks were comped," she said. "Ollie says you drink free all night."

"Too bad it's a school night," Greta said, sipping her pinot noir.

They all ordered the fish special, a Tuscan baked cod, except Murph, who had a burger. When the waitress disappeared, Pam turned to him. "So you lived in the city?"

Sandy nodded. "Yup. Brooklyn. Was terrific for a while, but I was ready to come home."

"What drew you back?" Pam asked.

"Love. My ex's dad lives in the city. We met at his theater, but she lived here, so I followed her home."

"Did you build your club?" Greta asked.

"Sort of. It was a run-down event venue that we had to gut, then pretty much rebuild from scratch."

"According to what I hear, you get wonderful musicians," Pam said.

Sandy smiled. "We've been lucky. The club's a work in progress."

"Bullshit," Murph scoffed. "It's the most successful music venue in the northeast."

"Murph's prone to exaggeration," he said.

Murph gazed from Pam to Greta. "Google him and the club. You'll see what I'm talking about."

"Are we putting you out with our event?" Pam asked, surprised at the contrasting images of the man beside her.

"Not at all. Sandy's does a lot of charity events. Besides, Thursdays are slow. The band we'd booked was happy to switch to a weekend night," Sandy said.

As they discussed the fundraiser, their dinner arrived and conversation was lively throughout, with Greta and Murph flirting shamelessly and Pam and Sandy acutely aware of each other. Occasionally, their hands touched or their knees and legs under the table. Each time, Pam gulped, the flood of sensations threatening to overwhelm her. As they shared two Portuguese flans, Sandy reached over under the table grasped her hand in his.

Pam gasped as her cheeks turned crimson. "You okay?" Greta asked, concern reflected in her eyes.

Pam forced a smile, withdrawing her hand from his, but not before he squeezed hers gently. "Fine. I think the flan went down the wrong way. You know, it's getting late. We'd better ask for the check."

"Already taken care of," Sandy said, voice low and sexy beside her.

"But…can't we contribute?" She dared not meet his eyes.

Sandy winked at Greta. "You ladies can pick it up next time, right, Murph?"

"Won't get an argument from me." Murph grinned as he watched the interplay between his boss and Pam Morgan.

"Okay, well. Thank you." Pam waited for him to stand so she could slide out of the enclosed space.

Reluctant to move away from her, Sandy took his time getting up. When he did, he stood at the edge of the bench, forcing Pam to rub against him as she stepped by. She held her breath and squeezed by, electricity crackling between them. The four headed out together, but the men were waylaid at the door by Oliver Silva. Pam and Greta waved goodbye and stepped out.

*****

"So those are two hot guys," Greta said on the drive home.

"Oh?" Pam was relieved to find her breath had finally gone back to normal.

"Oh nothing. If the chemistry had been any hotter between you two, you'd have exploded the table. You've been holding out on me, girl. How long have you been seeing Mr. Hotty?"

"Not long, and we're not seeing each other. We're neighbors who've bumped into each other a couple of times. You're dreaming if you think there's chemistry there."

"Keep telling yourself that, babe. But he's hot for you, and you're gaga over him."

"Stop!" Pam said, her sore cheek throbbing. She realized as they headed into town that she hadn't felt any pain even while eating. *Was it the wine or the company? Yikes, how will I get through this event with him lurking around? Mr. Hotty indeed!*

*****

"So what was that, boss?" Murph asked as they hopped into the truck.

"A great dinner. At least mine was good. How 'bout your burger?"

"You know damn well what I mean. You were playing pussy foot with Miz Morgan all night."

Sandy gave him a wry look. "Pussy foot?"

Murph laughed. "You know you dig her."

"She's interesting. Yes."

"And scared shitless of you, man."

"That's 'cause she thinks I have a reputation."

"Which you kinda do."

Sandy chuckled. "Well, it's a moot point because she's made it very clear she wants nothing to do with me."

"When has that ever stopped you?"

"We'll see," Sandy said, pulling into the club lot next to Murph's car. "See you later."

As he drove home, Sandy thought about Pam's soft, smooth skin, her scent of orange and something else he couldn't quite identify. *Intoxicating.* He couldn't remember when a woman had had such an effect on him. Even with her swollen cheek and bandaged forehead, she was beautiful. Quite the loveliest woman he'd met in many years, maybe ever. They hadn't even kissed, but just thinking about her made his cock grow hard. *Too bad she wants nothing to do with you, buddy.*

Chapter 9

Pam saw two private clients Tuesday. She shared office space above Village Books with therapist Elise Nolan, who worked Monday, Wednesday, and Friday. It was late morning when her last client departed, so she decided to stroll down and pick up a sandwich at the Café to take home. As she pushed open the restaurant door, she bumped smack into Sandy Rodriguez's chest. "Oh!" she said, arms flailing as she fought to regain her balance.

He grabbed hold of her waist, steadying her. "Hey, I was just thinking about you."

Beet red and flustered, Pam stepped back outside, down the Café stoop. "Oh?"

"I was thinking I don't have your number in case I want to call."

She frowned. "For what reason?"

He watched her, repressing a grin. "Oh, I don't know. If we had questions about your fundraiser setup or—"

Pam shook her head, stepping aside to let other patrons enter the Café. She felt like a twelve-year-old schoolgirl and an idiot to boot. "I'm sorry. Of course you should have it." She rummaged around in her purse, extracting a business card and handing it to him. "The number on it is my cell."

"Great, thanks," he said, his hand lingering on hers a trifle longer than necessary for the handoff. "You here for lunch?"

"Just grabbing a sandwich to eat up at the garden."

"Garden?"

"It's a long story."

"Well, why don't I grab something too, and we can eat together? Unless I'd be intruding?"

"But aren't you just leaving?"

"I was actually just passing by and saw a buddy through the window, so I went in to say hi. But I could use lunch." His expression open with not a hint of wolfishness, he looked especially delectable in an open-collared blue shirt and jeans.

Suddenly, Pam laughed. "Why not. Come on."

They both ordered sandwiches and drinks, for which he insisted on paying. As they exited the Café, she said," You didn't have to buy my lunch."

"Least I could do."

"For?"

"For scaring you silly every time we meet."

"Ha-ha. I'm just wary, that's all."

"Of me or men in general?"

She looked over at him, weighing the question. "Probably a little of both, if I'm being totally honest."

"Well, you don't have to be scared of me. We're friends, period."

Pam smiled. "Oh, is that what we are?"

"Your cheek looks better. And you look pretty. Those work clothes?"

Pam gazed down at her khakis and pale blue sweater that matched her eyes. Nothing special, but they were comfortable, like most of her work clothes. "Do friends tell friends they're pretty?"

He smiled. "Mine do."

"I'll bet," she said, realizing that now *she* was flirting. "Yes, I worked this morning. Private patients. I share an office with another therapist."

"Elise?"

"Yes, you know her?"

"I do." That was all she was going to get about his association with the pretty therapist. *No doubt an old girlfriend, like three-quarters of the women in town!*

"So here it is," she said as they reached the open field, now partially cleared and tilled. The future home of the community garden. In the north corner, a few makeshift benches had been erected from logs and four-by-six boards that would eventually form the sides of the raised beds.

He gazed around. "Haven't driven by here in a while. What is it?"

"It's going to be a community garden. It will be handicapped accessible and the beds high enough for people to garden in chairs, if that's more comfortable."

"Wow, cool idea. Yours?"

"Sort of. It's been a dream of mine since I started my practice in Maine. A way to honor our mom, who loved to garden. Never found the right spot in Portland, but this space called to me one day when my sister and I were walking. It's Mavis LaSalle's property, but she's donating it to the village. It also helps to have a wealthy father who enjoys nothing more than supporting his kids. He and Mavis are buddies, so he helped convince her, and he's also bankrolling start-up costs."

"Have the papers been signed?"

"No."

"Better not tell her you know me until they are."

"Don't be ridiculous. Everyone knows everyone in Horseshoe Crab Cove."

"I'm kidding, but I'm not one of Mavis's favorite people. Anyway, tell me about your dream."

As they ate, Pam told him about the garden and Kitty's plan. The conversation was easy and relaxed, and for a brief time, she forgot her insane attraction to the man sitting next to her. "We're having a community work day this Saturday. Hopefully, the tilling will be done and the top soil and manure delivered so we can build the raised beds."

"Happy to help. I bet I could get one or two of my brothers to help. Murph too."

Pam hesitated. Any help would be fantastic, but the fear of poking the bear and offending Mavis held her back. Finally, she said, "Of course, we'd love it. Thank you. We're assembling around nine, but come anytime. My dad's providing food and drinks all day."

"Is your patroness coming?" he asked.

"Probably not. We're into prime wedding season, and I hear Mavis is booked solid till Thanksgiving."

"Always."

"Besides, this is a community project, bigger than petty jealousies and resentments. Everyone in the community who wants to should be involved."

He smiled, that gorgeous, knock-me-over-with-a-feather smile that went right through her. "That's the spirit. Hey, I'd love to sit here all afternoon, but I've gotta get going. Deliveries coming in an hour, and Murph's off today."

As they strolled back, he said, "I'm glad we're friends."

Pam turned to him, trying to read his expression. "Me too," she said finally. "This is me." She pointed to her car.

"Hey, I don't suppose you'd like to have a friendly dinner sometime?"

"Sure, why not," she said, surprised at herself.

"I'll call you." He pulled her card from his pocket and twirled it in his fingers.

"Great." As she turned away, Pam smiled from ear to ear. Somehow, she knew that Sandy Rodriguez had not needed to ask for her number. Something told her he probably already had it or could get it with the snap of his fingers.

CHAPTER 10

Thursday morning, Pam, Gail, and their father sat at breakfast discussing their weekend plans. Pam had come over early to chat about the garden project. Even though the conversation had been amiable, she found herself giving short, clipped replies to their queries about Saturday's work day at the garden. Finally, Richard said, "You okay, sweetheart?"

"Fine, Dad, why?" Pam answered, feeling a headache brewing. She hopped up and poured a third cup of coffee, unusual for her.

"You don't sound fine," Gail said. "You're snapping at us, and you look like you just rolled out of the wrong side of the bed. Are you wearing that to work?"

"I don't have clients today," Pam said. "And what's the matter with what I'm wearing?" She gazed down at her clean, faded jeans over which she wore a navy cotton twin set.

"Well, for one thing, your sweater's wrinkled and that color makes you look like death. For another, your hair looks like you haven't combed it in a week."

"Now, now," their father said, frowning at Gail. "Pammie looks just fine. More than fine. She's my beautiful sunshine girl."

Pam smiled at her father. "Gail's right. I'm not your sunshine girl today, Dad. More like a shapeless gray storm cloud. Sorry, I feel a migraine coming on. I'm going to lie down in the den, if that's okay?"

"Of course, baby. I wish you'd stay here till you're fully recovered."

"I'm fine, Dad. Really." She grabbed her mug and breakfast things and headed for the kitchen.

As she settled in the den, a small room behind Richard's study, Pam knew the real reason for her foul mood. Yes, she was prone to tension headaches and there were a lot of details to work out for Saturday. Things had also been stressful at school Wednesday dealing with the aftermath of the boys' suspensions and the reaction to her injuries. Her cheek was no longer so sore but was an ugly black, blue, and yellow. All those factors were true, but if she were being honest, the real reason for her bad temper was that a certain handsome club owner hadn't phoned. She'd been so sure he'd phone to ask her out, but nothing. She found herself checking her phone every five minutes for missed calls. *This isn't me! Let it go,* she told herself as she collapsed on the sofa, closing her eyes.

Despite all the caffeine, she fell asleep, waking an hour later, groggy. The house was quiet as she wandered out to collect her things. She found Callie upstairs vacuuming and asked where everyone was. "Your dad's down at the stables, Gail went to town, and Weezie's probably down with the horses. Haven't seen either of your brothers today."

"Thanks, Cal. I'm heading home."

"Can I get you anything before you go?"

Gail smiled. "Aside from a new face, I'm all set. Thanks. See ya."

On the drive home, she decided a run would do her good. After changing, she grabbed a water bottle. A warm day, there was a lovely breeze off the water as she started out. She decided to take the southern route that ran parallel to the Loop Trail, a dirt path that circled around the peninsula. When she neared the Loop, she hopped onto the dirt trail and had gone a little over a mile when she saw a lone runner headed her way. A man, he was tall and well built. As he emerged from the shadows, she recognized him. *Shit! Nowhere to hide!*

"Hey," Sandy said as they met. "Perfect day for a run, huh?"

"It's nice, yes." *God, the man looks great in spandex, and those legs!*

"How have you been? The face looks much better."

"If you like yellow and brown skin. Well… I should probably keep going," she said.

"Me too. Hey, before you go." He reached out and took hold of her arm.

Pam flinched. "Yes?" she said, wriggling free of his grasp.

"Sorry, I just wanted to say that I've been meaning to call you. We've been real busy this week, and I didn't know when I'd get a free moment.

"I can imagine."

"But I wonder… I mean, I was going to call and see if you're free for an early dinner tomorrow night? Fridays I have more help. We have a group that night, but I can go in later and Murph can hold down the fort. So what do you say? Are you free for a friendly dinner?"

Pam wanted to ask if this invitation was simply spur-of-the-moment upon seeing her. *Would he really have called?* Despite these questions, she answered, "Yes, that'd be fine. What time?"

"Pick you up at five thirty? Is that too early?"

"Perfect. I have to be up early the next morning for the garden work."

Sandy grinned. "Okay, see you then. It'll be someplace casual, so don't dress up." Without another word, he ran off, leaving her watching his long loping retreat.

What did you just do, Pam Morgan? Friendly indeed! Her legs like jelly, she started off again, taking deep breaths.

CHAPTER 11

Work continued to be stressful to the point that Pam was considering quitting. Jared Cochran's family had taken out a restraining order against Mickey Parks. Neither boy was back in school, but fear gripped her every morning as she drove into the school lot. She had witnessed fights before, even broken them up, but never been caught in the crossfire. Her heart raced every time she received a call from a teacher or classroom. Friday was a quiet day, but she still left school with frazzled nerves, Greta at her side.

"It's gotten to you, hasn't it?" her friend said.

Pam nodded, tears in her eyes. "I'm not sure I can keep doing this, and that makes me feel like such a coward. I mean, it was just being in the wrong place at the wrong time. It could happen at the market, at Averills, just walking down Main Street."

Greta nodded. "Exactly. So the job is just a job, and you're good at it. Give it time. It only happened four days ago."

"Maybe I'm better sticking to private practice."

"What happened Monday can just as easily happen in a therapist's office."

"I know." Pam gave her a wan smile.

"Hey, want to grab some dinner and drink a lot of wine? That'll put a better perspective on all this."

"Or just temporarily blot it out only to have it coming crashing back along with a monster hangover."

"Well then, maybe moderate drinking and a good dinner? Saves me having to think about cooking," Greta said.

"Thanks but I can't. I have plans."

"Oh?"

"A friendly dinner, that's all."

"I knew it! You're having a date with Mr. Dreamy! I am so jealous. And his friend never so much as called!"

"His friend has a steady girlfriend," Pam said. "And it is not a date. Just dinner with a friend."

"Keep telling yourself that, dearie. Have a fun night, and I'll see you in the morning. By the way, I roped my brother into coming, so one more pair of hands for the garden."

"Thank you so much," Pam said. Before going home, she wanted to stop in and talk to Kitty about organizing the volunteers. When they'd spoken yesterday, Kitty assured her she would have a plan.

When she arrived at Village Hardware, Kitty was with a client, so Pam sat on a bench, enjoying the warm afternoon sun and closed her eyes. Immediately, the impending evening sprang to mind, but before she had time to begin obsessing, a voice called her back to the present.

"Hey, Pam."

She opened her eyes to find her sister's handsome fiancé, Tim Miller, standing over her, his dark hair flecked with sawdust. Affectionately referred to as "Heathcliff of Horseshoe Crab Cove," he was less the image of Brontë's hero as he was of the young Laurence Olivier who had played him.

"Tim! Hi. You caught me."

"Long day?"

"Something like that. I'm having a sort of job crisis, wondering if I'm in the wrong profession."

He studied her face. "Gail told me what happened. You okay?"

"Physically yes, mentally no."

"Well, speaking as someone who did a one eighty career wise, there *is* life on the other side."

"There's a lot of guilt thinking about leaving."

"Taking a break doesn't mean you can't go back if you want."

She nodded, surprised to be having this conversation with Tim, with whom she had rarely exchanged more than a few words. "You're right. I'll figure it out."

"And you've got a good safety net here. People who care about you."

"You're right about that. My dad would like nothing better than for me to quit. We're very spoiled."

Tim smiled, the glorious smile that made women's hearts beat faster. "You guys are lucky. We all are, in fact."

Kitty's door opened, and her clients departed. Pam said, "Good to see you, Tim. I've got to go. Thanks for the wise words."

"Anytime. See you tomorrow morning."

"Yes," she said. "And thanks for that too."

"Wouldn't miss it for the world," he said, heading into the hardware store. "Got the family coming too."

She waved to Kitty and went to meet her.

*****

I really need to stand on my own two feet, Pam thought as she showered and selected clothes for her dinner with Sandy. Even as she began fundraising efforts for the garden, Richard Morgan had insisted on paying all upfront costs from Kitty Bannister's fee to site clearing and tilling, the top soil, fertilizers, tools, and lumber for the garden. Tomorrow, a garden shed would be delivered to store all the tools and equipment on site courtesy of Morgan Enterprises.

"Everything's a tax deduction," he father told her continually, but it was time to have others contribute to Laura's Community Garden. She had just decided on the name today on her way home from Kitty's. It was fitting and helped to keep the mother she barely remembered in her heart in some small way.

Sandy had said casual, so she selected black skinny jeans and a pale blue shirred top that flattered her slender frame, hugging her body in all the right places. She chose silver earrings and a few delicate silver bangles at her wrist, then brushed her hair, leaving it loose around her shoulders. Pam rarely used makeup but decided a little lipstick wouldn't hurt. When she surveyed herself in the bedroom's full-length mirror, she decided she looked fine for a friendly dinner and grabbed a denim jacket in case it was cool.

When the doorbell rang, she peeked out, expecting to see his truck. Instead, a silver Audi convertible sat in the driveway. *A man of constant surprises*, she thought, going to the door.

"Hey, all set?" he asked.

"I am. Is this okay for where we're going?"

He grinned, his eyes appraising every inch of her. "More than okay. But then you'd look more than okay in a burlap sack."

Pam smiled. "Which is a sight I hope never to see." She grabbed her purse and stepped out, shutting the door behind her.

"How do you like living here?" he asked.

"Love it. The Fergusons have been great. The house came furnished, which was so easy, but if I ask to have something removed to make room for my things, they get Kevin Averill out here the next day to move their stuff out." She referred to the son of Hank Averill, owner of Averill's General Store.

"Yeah? Kev does odd jobs for me too."

"At the club?"

"And the house."

He opened her door, and Pam slid in, her arm grazing his. He smelled of citrus and spices. Intoxicating! "Thank you," she managed with a tremulous voice. *Oh boy, how will I get through the next two hours?*

As the car purred to life and he backed out, she asked, "Where are we going?"

"I thought we'd go to Bluewater, unless you have somewhere else you'd prefer?"

"Bluewater's perfect."

They chatted about their day and various innocuous topics on the drive to Southport. Sandy had made a reservation, so they were ushered in to a table by the waiter as soon as they arrived.

"Have you been here before?"

She nodded. "A couple of times."

"It's one of my favorites. Great seafood and not stuffy."

She smiled. "So you don't like stuffy?"

"Not especially. You?"

"Not that it isn't fun to dress up sometimes, but if I can go in jeans, I'm a happy camper."

The waitress came by and recited the specials, then took their drink order. Pam ordered white wine and Sandy a beer. They consulted their menus for a minute or two. When she set hers down, he did as well. "So tell me about Pam Morgan. Where's life taken you so far?"

"Not fair," she said. "I was going to ask you that same question."

He grinned. "Later."

"Well, I was born in Singapore, but I don't remember it. I was only nine months old when Dad and Mom decided to come back to the States. They bought a huge piece of land in Maine, just outside of Portland, and started an organic farm. It was Mom's dream, and it was beautiful. Two of my siblings were born in Maine, but she got sick when she was pregnant with my youngest brother, Wolfie. Cancer. She refused treatment until after he was born, and by then, it was too late. I only have vague memories of her reading to us and a few images of her working in the gardens.

"My dad raised us with a succession of nannies, most of them great. It wasn't easy for him. I'm a product of great public schools, and I went to college in New York City. Got my graduate degree there too. At that time, my aunt Cherie lived in the city, so I stayed with her. She's since moved to Maine but is always threatening to go back to the city. Enough bio?"

"What college?"

"Barnard, then NYU."

"Impressive."

Pam smiled. "Not really."

The waitress appeared with their drinks and took their orders. Pam ordered the swordfish special, and he ordered sea bass. When she disappeared, Pam said, "Now it's your turn."

"Not nearly as interesting or exotic. Grew up here. My folks are terrific. I was kind of their wild child, so they sent me to boarding school."

"Oh? Where?"

"Middlesex, then to college in Connecticut. I majored in English, if you can believe it. Lot of good it did me. I came home. Taught two years at the high school, then hightailed it to the city. Got my MBA, met Lolly, and we came home."

"Did you know her growing up?"

"No, she grew up in the city. They started coming here summers and bought the property Mavis now owns. Do you know any of Mavis's other kids?"

Pam shook her head. "Although I understand her daughter Marla is local?"

He grinned. "Her band plays regularly at the club. She still speaks to me."

"Divorce is hard, isn't it? Especially in a small town."

He shrugged. "Life goes on."

Pam met his eyes and for an instant saw sadness. "And you have a beautiful little girl."

"Yup."

"The summer you came to Maine to work for Dad must've been just before college, right?"

"After my freshman year, actually. One of my professors knew your dad and got me the job."

"So you were at Yale. Must have been Murray Reiss, right?"

He smiled. "The very same. Does your dad still see him?"

"Murray passed away two years ago. Heart attack, very sudden."

"I'm sorry. I didn't know that. Guess I'm behind in reading my alumni mags. He was a great guy."

"Yes, he was. He and Dad were very close friends. Aunt Cherie says Murray was there for him when Mom died. Says he'd have never made it back if it weren't for Murray and his wife, Anne. They dropped everything and came to Maine when Mom died. They stayed for six months, then came almost every weekend for years."

"Yup, sounds like Professor Reiss."

The waitress served their entrees, and they both ordered a second drink. When she departed, Pam said, "Thank you for this. I'm enjoying myself."

"Me too. Friends?"

Pam smiled. "Friends." As she took her first bite of fish, she looked up, finding him staring at her. "Uh-oh, have I dribbled down my front?" she asked, gazing down.

"Nope. Just waiting to see if you like the swordfish."

"It's excellent. Yours?"

"Yup. So you left out any mention of your personal life. Boyfriends?"

She looked up, trying to gauge his intent, but saw the same open friendliness, not a hint of guile or sarcasm. "Not many. I dated a few people in high school, but they ended up just friends. Then there was a guy when I was in college, but that fizzled out. He found his true love and broke it off. I was hurt, but it was ultimately fine. We weren't compatible."

"Because?"

"Because he loved things that I avoid like the plague. Country clubs, shopping, exclusive resorts. He was always trying to take me shopping for clothes. He loved suggesting what he thought would suit me, usually in shades of lime green and hot pink."

"Seriously?"

"Seriously. Anyway, he's now an investment banker, filthy rich, married with one or two kids. They send Christmas cards."

"Wow. Is he your age?"

"No, he was five years older, out of grad school, when we met." Pam set down her fork. "Enough about me. What about your love life? Much more interesting, from all accounts."

He shrugged. "Not really. I dated in high school and college like everyone else. Then there was Lolly. She and I… What can I say about us? There was a definite spark, but by the time we moved back here, we were more like brother and sister. We gave it the old college try, but things deteriorated. Then Maisie was born, and things went from bad to worse. My behavior didn't help. I'm not proud of the affairs."

"Affairs?"

"Mostly one-night stands. More than a few."

"But why? How could you?"

"Anything I say will sound like an excuse."

"Try me."

"The best explanation is probably loneliness. I don't blame Loll, but she disappeared after Maisie was born."

"Sounds like motherhood can be all-consuming."

"I know, I get it, but I was young and foolish and selfish, I guess."

Pam gazed over at his handsome features clouded by the darkness of his self-critique. "You know what…enough about the past. Tell me about Sandy's and how you've gotten so successful."

"Luck and persistence. Now tell me about your garden."

They spent the remainder of the meal in easy conversation about a number of present-day subjects. When the waitress brought the check, he grabbed it.

As they walked out, his hand touched the small of her back, guiding her through the door. Friends they might be, but Pam felt the now-familiar shiver of sensation at his nearness. "I'm sorry this has to end so early," he said, voice close to her ear.

"Me too," she said, turning to him, just as he turned to her. Their lips grazed each other's and lingered, a soft fleeting kiss. Then they were next to his car, his hand on the door handle, their eyes locked on one another. "This feels like a danger zone," she whispered.

"Not for me," he said, stepping back and reaching around to open her door. As she slipped by him, she felt his lips on her neck. Just one kiss, but that was all it took. When he came around and slid into the driver's seat, the door had barely shut when their lips found each other with a deep, lasting kiss, their tongues hungry for each other, bodies moving as close as was possible over the car's console.

Practiced hands cupped her breasts, then slipped under her sweater, nudging the lace of her bra aside to stroke and tease. Pam moaned, arching toward him, lost in a whirling sea of sensation as her arms encircled his neck. Suddenly, he stopped. "Hey, my friend, this better not go any further here in the Bluewater parking lot. It's not even dark."

Breathing a huge sigh, Pam let go and slumped back against her seat. "I lied."

"Excuse me?" he said.

"I lied to you. I don't want to be friends."

"Why not?"

"Because I want this and more… I mean, I want to be friends, but I want more than friendship."

"Well, you picked an awkward time and place, babe. Can I take a rain check?"

"No… Yes…I don't know."

"Listen, I wasn't watching the time. I've got to get to the club. Want to come along?"

"I really shouldn't. I have to get up really early, and there's so much to do."

"Just for an hour. I promised to introduce tonight's group, then I'm pretty free for an hour or so. I can drive you home, then come back and close up."

CHAPTER 12

As they drove north, Pam's fingers caressed the back of his head. Now that she'd had a taste of him, she couldn't keep her hands off. Then they walked into the club, and he was swallowed up, Pam pushed aside as they prepared for the evening's entertainment. She found a quiet table in the corner and watched. In his element, Sandy gave directions and greeted guests and band members with the easy charm that had made him and the club such a huge success. He introduced the group, the Muddy River Blues, then disappeared into the crowd.

The band was terrific, the dance floor full, but Pam was tired and ready to go. Stifling a yawn, she was just considering whether to call one of her sisters or Uber for a ride home when he appeared beside her. "Ready? Unless you want to dance?"

The band began a slow bluesy number, and she said, "Maybe just one."

Sandy held out his hand, and she took it, allowing him to lead her onto the dance floor. As he drew her into his arms, she gasped, wondering if she'd ever breathe again. Their bodies fit perfectly as they moved in synch, his arousal evident against her jeans. Pam wrapped both arms around his neck and gave herself to the music and his embrace. Sandy trailed soft kisses down her neck as he whispered, "You smell incredible, babe."

When the music stopped, their bodies continued to move, locked in their own private world. "I think I'd better get you out of here," he whispered. "We can go out the back."

"My purse," she said, gazing languidly up at him.

After collecting her purse and jacket, they slipped out the back onto a private section of porch at the rear of the building. "Where are we?" she said.

"Private dining area. We don't use it much. Needs work."

She could hear the ocean just around the corner, waves lapping at the club's southern deck. "It's nice."

"Yeah, it's nice," he said, his lips capturing hers.

Weak kneed and faint when the kiss ended, Pam was suffused with warmth and intense desire. She began kissing his neck and cheeks, her fingers tracing his strong jawline. She ached to touch every part of him.

"You sure about this, Pam?"

She nodded. "Uh-huh."

"'Cause there'll be no stopping it soon."

"If you stop, I'll scream," she said, moving her body against him, the feel of his cock rendering her delirious with wanting him.

He slipped his fingers into her pants, moving between her legs to her moist center. "Oh, babe, you're amazing. He unbuttoned her jeans and slipped them and her panties off. The evening breeze sent shivers over her bare skin. As his hand slipped between her legs again, his thumb found her clit and his fingers went deeper, taking her over the edge to a powerful blinding orgasm. Her legs threatened to buckle, but he caught her. "What do you want, baby?"

"More, I want more, and I want you inside me," she whispered, heedless of the fact that they could be discovered at any moment.

In answer, he unzipped his jeans and slipped on a condom he retrieved from his wallet. "You sure?" he asked, gazing down at her in the moonlight.

Pam kissed him deeply before breaking free. "What do you think?"

He lifted her legs, wrapping them around him as he carried her backward to rest against the wall. Then his cock found her warm slick center. He thrust a few inches at first, then deeper and deeper as Pam arched forward to meet him. "Oh, baby," he groaned, as they rose higher and higher to a crashing simultaneous climax.

Pam felt like a limp rag doll in his arms as they rested in the darkness. He kissed her forehead, then her nose before grazing her lips. "What the hell was that?" he whispered, voice gruff and full of emotion.

"Seemed like we went a bit beyond the friends thing," she said.

"Ya think?"

They both laughed, clinging to each other for several minutes until he said, "While I'd like nothing better than to hold you like this all night, I'm gonna have to take you home, babe."

Pam nodded, feeling bereft as he withdrew and set her down. They dressed quickly, then she gathered her things and they headed for the car. Quiet on the drive back, Pam wondered if it had all been a dream.

He walked her to the door and pulled her into his arms for a deep, lingering kiss. "Thanks, babe. I had a really good time."

She smiled up at him. "Me too. Night."

"See you tomorrow."

"Yes."

As she closed the door behind him, Pam grinned, then blanched. *What have I done?*

CHAPTER 13

The day dawned clear, bright, and warm. Pam met Kitty a little after six to go over details and plan tasks for each work crew. Some would be building bed sides, others would be grading, hauling dirt and fertilizer, some arranging garden structures and erecting fences. "What do you think?" she asked Kitty after they walked the property.

"I think it's doable if we get able bodies and they stay organized. If you're getting the numbers you expect and they keep on task, we should get the beds in, fences up, and the two test beds planted. We might get a start on planting the sensory beds too." At each end of the garden, they'd planned a test bed, one flowers, the other vegetables and their companion plants. They had situated the flower bed near the entrance to the garden and the vegetables at the far end. Lucy's arbor would serve as the garden entrance once the fencing was up. On either side of the arbor, long narrow beds would be planted with herbs and plants of many hues, scents, and textures.

"God bless Abe Burrell," Kitty said. "He did a great job with clearing and tilling. The ground's level and ready for the beds." Abe, a local farmer, had also volunteered to work in the afternoon after he'd done the milking and his own garden chores.

"Yes, and he charged us next to nothing. Just enough to cover his gas, I'm betting."

Kitty nodded. "He's a sweetie. So I hear you corralled some of the Rodriguez men. Talk about gorgeous, but do they get their hands dirty?"

Pam swallowed hard, remembering the hands of a certain Rodriguez man and how they'd felt on her body less than twelve hours ago. Then she grinned at Kitty. "I guess we'll find out."

"Seriously, do you know them well?" Kitty asked as they unloaded equipment from her pickup.

"None of them except Sandy. He's a friend and says he's bringing his brothers, or at least one of them."

"I hope it's Raffi," Kitty said, a dreamy look in her eye.

Pam smiled. "Do I detect an attraction there?"

"Have you ever seen him?"

Pam shook her head.

"Well, get ready, 'cause he's swoon-worthy and doesn't he know it too. Not to mention filthy rich."

"Isn't he the attorney?"

"Yup. Hey here comes your Dad. Talk about gorgeous *and* the man of the hour. Hey, Mr. Morgan!" Kitty called, waving as Pam turned to spy her dad, Weezie, and Gail laden with boxes and bags.

"Mornin', ladies! And there'll be no Mr. Morgans here today. Richard or 'hey you' will do just fine."

Kitty laughed. "What've you got there, Richard?"

"Breakfast. Lucy and Callie are stopping at the Café and bringing big urns of coffee, hot water, lemonade, and iced tea. They'll be here soon."

"Rich and Gus are right behind us with the tables," Gail said as Gus Casey pulled his truck onto the field.

Kitty went to direct the two men on table placement, and Pam helped lay out food. One table had been reserved for the garden blueprints and held a basket of work clothes and gloves in all sizes. In addition to the tables, Rich, Gus, and Dennis Farrell, the farm's assistant trainer, unloaded cases of water and four large trash barrels. As Pam watched them carry the water by, she sighed. "One day and so much plastic. The well's in and working, but this seemed easier today."

"Much easier," Gail said, arm around her sister. "Take a deep breath, sis. This is all your doing, and you should be super proud."

Pam rested her head on Gail's shoulder. "I'll be prouder at sundown when the work's completed."

Soon, droves of people began arriving from school, the village and their families. There were many Millers, Tim's family, as well as Lolly, her sister Marla, and members of Marla's band, The Cherry Pickers. As people arrived, Kitty and Pam quickly assigned them to work crews. Gus had already been put in charge of fencing, and he and his crew were working steadily around the perimeter, sinking metal stakes, unrolling miles of heavy-duty wire fencing and securing each length to the ground and stakes. Another crew was building the bed boxes, then setting them in place. By the time the Rodriguez gang arrived shortly before nine, the property was buzzing with activity.

Spying Sandy, Pam paused to greet him, clipboard in hand as she approached the group. "Welcome!"

Sandy gave her a secret smile, and Pam blushed, hoping it just looked like overheating. He stepped forward. "Let me do quick intros, then you can put us to work. Our sister Milania has to work, but she said she'd come over later and bring food. For now you've got the rest of my crew—Mike, Vincent, Raffi, and Sonia." One by one, each said hello and shook Pam's hand. All had dark hair and eyes as beautiful as their brother's.

As Raffi shook her hand, he said, "You must be really special, Pam Morgan. My brother was relentless. We had no option but to show up." There was more than a hint of mischief in his dark eyes as he looked from Pam to Sandy and back again.

They were interrupted by Kitty, who called, "Hey, Rodriguez family. We've got just the job for you." Pam noticed she directed her remarks to Raffi, who, after teasing his brother, was grinning from ear to ear.

Sandy gave him a shove and said, "Lead on Kitty."

They grabbed work gloves and followed Kitty toward huge piles of loam and fertilizer, wheelbarrows and garden carts lined up beside them. Sandy lingered behind long enough to say, "Great job. This is amazing. I'm not sure the village has seen anything like this since we built the school playground."

Pam gave him a shy smile. "Thanks. I'm so grateful for your family's help. I see people from school coming in, so I'd better go. See you later."

He reached over and took her hand, giving it a gentle squeeze. "Count on it."

Greta and some of her colleagues had arrived, and were headed her way. As she gazed around, deciding where to put them, her stepmother came up. "What a turnout," Lucy said. "You must be thrilled!"

Pam smiled at her. "I am."

"Just a quick warning before you greet your friends. Lolly saw your interchange with the Rodriguez family and especially your moment with Sandy. It's not my business, but if there's something going on between you, you might want to keep it low-key today. Thank goodness Mavis has already signed the papers, right?"

"Yesterday," Pam said, looking at Lucy. "Was it that obvious?"

"'Fraid so, but no worries. Go see your friends. I'm checking on the food supplies, then back to my flower bed work. Such fun!"

Mortified, Pam went to greet Greta and the others.

CHAPTER 14

Shortly before noon, Richard, Weezie, and Callie arrived with boxed lunches and coolers full of drinks. Milania Rodriguez brought boxes of cookies, brownies, and other desserts from the Café where she worked. As soon as she set them down, she found Pam.

"Hey, I'm Milly, Sandy's sister. Where do you need me?"

"Are you sure you can spare the time?" she asked Sandy's pretty youngest sibling. Milly's dark shoulder-length hair was pulled back in a ponytail, her curvaceous figure evident in denim capris and a skintight Crab Café T-shirt. Her dark blue eyes twinkled. "My brother was *most* insistent. Haven't heard that much urgency in his voice since he needed help after Maisie's birth."

"Well, you're all very kind," Pam said, knowing she was once again turning bright red. "Why don't you join your brothers and Sonia with the beds for now?"

When the lunches were laid out, Kitty rang a bell and called, "Lunch break!" in a surprisingly loud voice.

As people stopped work and came to get food, Pam and Kitty grabbed drinks and went to sit near the shed to regroup and determine where they needed to redirect for the afternoon. Kitty plunked down beside her. "So where are we?"

Pam gazed around at rows of assembled beds, some already filled with rich loam planting mixture. "Miraculously, the fence is almost complete. Gus says he'll see it through, then he and Dennis have to head back to the farm."

"The arbor's ready to go in," Kitty said. The wrought iron arbor and trellis lay nearby. Extra-wide and double gates had been added by Coop Merrick.

"It's amazing how far along we are," Pam said, gazing in front of them.

"Many hands," Kitty said, "especially when the many hands are strong, able-bodied, and gorgeous."

Pam chuckled, watching her sister Weezie flirt with Raffi. "I don't think looks have anything to do with it."

"Doesn't your sister know that Raffi is mine?" Kitty whispered, giggling.

Pam poked her as her cousin Kyle Morgan, village veterinarian, and his fiancée, Harriet Winthrop, Lucy's sister, approached. "We've got chicken salad, tuna, veggie hummus, or ham," he said, flashing the Morgan grin. "Uncle Dick sent us to make sure our fearless leaders didn't starve."

Pam smiled at her cousin. "I'll take chicken salad. Thanks, guys." She accepted the box, which contained a sandwich wrap, chips, and an apple.

"Tuna'd be great," Kitty said as Harriet handed her a box.

"Gotta get back to our delivering duties. You're doing a great job, cuz," he said. "Can we get you anything else?"

"Thanks, we're good," Pam said.

"You are so lucky," Kitty said. "What an amazing family you have."

"Yes, I am." Pam leaned back against the shed, taking a bite of the delicious wrap.

They talked a few minutes more, then Kitty stood. "Gotta check on the plants. They were delivered an hour ago. Your stepmother and her friends have already planted half the flowers, but we don't want the rest wilting in the sun."

Pam finished her sandwich and was just about to rise when Sandy found her, sliding down to sit beside her. "Great job, boss."

Without thinking Pam leaned her head against his shoulder. "Thanks. Halfway there."

"That feels nice," he said, reaching down to take her hand.

"But probably a mistake at this particular moment." Lolly passed by with the group in charge of the arbor, and Pam sat up straight. "I've already been warned against public displays of affection, and look at us."

"Doesn't bother me a bit," he said, standing and offering her his hand, which she took, allowing his strong arm to help her up.

She smiled, gazing over to meet his beautiful dark eyes. "Well, time to get to work."

"Love to make another date soon," he whispered in her ear.

"One step at a time," she said hurrying away before she did something she'd really regret, *like flinging myself at him!*

Around three, the test beds were completed, and Pam was working on the sensory one near the entrance to the garden. Gail worked beside her as they carefully planted seedlings according to Kitty's blueprint. Her sister looked over at the arbor. "Is the sign ready?"

"Next week. Dad insisted on ordering from his guy in Portland."

"It's fitting, you know, Mom's name, but also something of Dad's and our new life with Lucy's generous gift."

"You're right," Pam said. "Mom would be so pleased, wouldn't she? I wish I remembered more about her. It seems like every year, more of my memories of her fade."

"Me too," Gail said.

"And Rich and Ava don't like to talk about her. It's almost as if it's too painful, and they can't bring themselves to—"

"What the hell do you think you're doing?"

The sisters turned to find Lolly LaSalle glaring down at them. "Excuse me?" Pam asked.

"My mother's made this project possible, and what does she do?" Lolly pointed a finger at Pam. "Hops into bed with my ex. You're screwing him, aren't you?"

One glance at her sister, who had turned white and was trembling, and Gail sprang up. "Now hold on, Lolly. This is neither the time nor the place."

"This was my land until yesterday," the angry woman said. "So I'll be the judge of when's the right time and place."

Lucy and Harriet hurried over, and Lucy took hold of her business partner's arm. "Come on, Loll. Everyone's tired."

Pam gazed around, grateful that only a handful of people were witnessing this nightmare. Then she stood, straight and tall, a good six inches taller than Lolly LaSalle. "I can see that you're upset, Ms. LaSalle. I'm sorry about that. I also have work to do. My private life and whatever wild assumptions you might have about it have nothing to do with what we're doing here. If you have a problem with me, I'm happy to speak with you another time, but right now, I'm going to continue planting. Excuse me." Chin up, she turned away and knelt down, resuming her place next to the bed. Shaking, she took deep breaths, endeavoring to refocus on the flat of herbs to her side.

"Come on Loll, we need help with the arbor. It's time," Lucy said as Harriet and the others lifted the structure, preparing to move it to its permanent location.

"You okay, sis?" Gail whispered as the others, including Lolly, moved away.

"No, but let's keep working. No time to fall apart now."

Workers drifted in and out, but as the skeleton crew cleaned and raked late in the day, phase one of the garden was completed. Thirty raised beds were filled and ready to plant, the property was fenced and gated, the pathways were cleared and tamped down, covered with three inches of pea stone. Tools were stowed, and two garden beds bloomed with new life.

They fed the remaining crew dinner, huge platters of Salters barbecue, salads, corn, and bread, and afterwards, people hugged and said goodbye. Harriet and Kyle were among the last to go. "You okay, cuz?" he asked Pam.

She peered at him, puzzled.

"Harriet told me about the scene. Don't let it mar this amazing day."

It had been three minutes out of an otherwise full and deeply satisfying day, but the trauma of Lolly's confrontation had hit her hard. Pam hugged him. "Thanks, Kyle. I'm sure trying."

Sandy and his brothers had left before dinner, so she wasn't sure if he'd heard about Lolly. *No matter, I'm exhausted. Home. Bed.*

CHAPTER 15

"Hey, your girl did good, didn't she?" Murph said as Sandy arrived at the club.

Too tired to correct the "your girl" comment, Sandy simply said, "It's going to be a great resource for the village." He slumped down onto a barstool. It had been a long time since he'd worked as hard as he had today. "All set for tonight?"

"Yup. That was quite a scene with your ex, huh? Poor Pam."

"What the hell are you talking about?"

"I hear she pretty much attacked her."

"What? Why?"

"You, of course. Guess Ms. LaSalle's not quite over you."

Blood pressure rising, Sandy said, "What exactly did you hear?"

Murph gave his thirdhand account ending with "I guess Pam stood up to her, but it couldn't have been fun. Probably put a damper on the day for her."

"Geez," Sandy said, pulling out his phone. Pam's phone went straight to voicemail. Like a caged animal, he began to pace. "So we've got the band starting at eight, then the food and all. I could just—"

"Boss, if you want to go, go. We can do it. The Dreads don't care who introduces them, and Gary and Suzie have the food. Their roadies'll help with setup and takedown."

"You sure?"

"We've got this—go!"

Sandy ran to the truck and drove down the coast toward home. He didn't know what he intended to do, but he had to see her. He went by the garden first, but it was deserted, shrouded in shadows. As he turned around in the lot, he shook his head, marveling at what they'd all accomplished in one day.

When he got to the house on Beach Road, the lights were out except on the second floor. He debated turning around, but then pulled into her drive and hopped out. *I'll just see if she's okay. Then I'll go.*

He rang the doorbell. Soon, lights switched on in the front hall, and the front stoop was illuminated as the door swung open. Barefoot, she wore a fuzzy blue bathrobe. Blue eyes blinked in surprise. "Sandy? Is everything okay?"

"Sorry, I just had to see you… To make sure you're okay."

She stared at him, puzzled and bleary-eyed. "But…but we said goodbye at the garden. Didn't I look okay?"

"I'm sorry. I woke you up."

"No, I was reading, but I have to admit I was missing the odd sentence or two. It was a long day." She gazed up and down the street, clearly wondering who might be watching. "Did you want to come in?"

"Only for a minute." He stepped inside, and she closed the door.

"If it's okay with you, let's talk upstairs. I'm about to keel over."

Now I know she's half asleep, he thought, following her up the narrow staircase. Pam flopped down on the mussed bed and pulled the covers up, indicating a chair nearby. "What's up?"

"I heard about the altercation with Lolly. I'm so sorry."

"No worries," she said. "As we've said many times, it's a small town. Bound to happen."

"I'll talk to her."

"No you won't." Pam reached out and took hold of his arm. "Please don't. Everyone was exhausted. Whatever she saw or thinks she saw, it probably just surprised her. I can understand that."

"We've been divorced for over four years. Time to move on."

"From what I hear some people never do." Pam regarded him. A day of hard physical labor had taken its toll. He was freshly showered and cleaner than when he'd left that afternoon, but he exuded weariness in body and spirit. "You look really tired. Want to lie down? No funny business."

He raised an eyebrow. "Funny business?"

"You know what I mean. Come on, what are friends for?" She moved aside and patted the bed beside her. Sandy lay down, and she threw a light quilt over them, sliding her arm down to cradle his head.

"This is a first," he said. "I really am sorry, you know."

"I know," she said as they both drifted off to sleep.

*****

When Pam woke, daylight streamed through the windows and the bed was empty. Assuming Sandy had departed in the night, she padded into the bathroom. On her way, the scent of bacon cooking wafted up from the kitchen. She took a quick shower, dressed, and went down to find him at the stove just removing crisp bacon from a skillet.

"This is a nice surprise," she said.

"The least I can do. How do you like your eggs? One or two?"

"Over easy. Two would be great." She slid onto a stool and watched him, a big grin on her face.

He smiled, meeting her eyes. "Is it okay that I'm doing this?"

"More than okay, and also a first for me."

"Eggs over easy?"

"No, a man in my kitchen cooking for me."

"After yesterday, someone should be waiting on you hand and foot."

She marveled at the curve of his shoulders, his amazing ass, the strong back relaxed as he flipped eggs and assembled breakfast. "I could get used to this," she said, then gasped, realizing she'd crossed a line. *We're talkin' about Mr. Love 'Em and Leave 'Em. This is probably one of his signature behaviors.*

"There's coffee, but I'm never sure with other people's machines."

She poured two mugs, set the cutlery and napkins on the table, and got two plates out of the cupboard. He slid the eggs and bacon on each, then pulled toast out of the oven, placing two perfect slices on each plate.

"How do you take your coffee?" she asked, pouring milk into her mug.

"Black, thanks. Here we go." He set the plates on the table and sat beside her.

She took up her fork, turning to him. "Thank you. I'm sure you've made a lot of women very happy doing this."

He grinned. "Only two before today."

"Really?"

"Lolly and Maisie. I'm not much of a caterer otherwise."

"You never cease to amaze me," she said.

"Good," he said. "Amazed is good."

*****

Breakfast dishes cleared, Pam said, "I hate to eat and run, but I've got to get changed and get to meeting. My dad counts on us, and I don't want to miss after all his help yesterday."

"You go to Quaker Meeting?"

She nodded. "At Lucy's sister Harriet's school. My parents started attending Meeting when we lived in Singapore. Churches are huge over there, with many services throughout the day and hundreds in the congregation at every one. There was only one Quaker service at Singapore Meeting. Their good friends invited them one Sunday, and that was it. We actually moved where we did in Maine to be close to the Portland Meeting. Of course I don't remember any of that. I was raised a Quaker. My parents were raised Episcopalians. Sorry, am I sharing too much?"

He smiled. "Not at all, but you'd better get going so you won't be late."

"You're right. Excuse me?"

"Of course. Go ahead. I'll do the dishes."

When she returned, the kitchen was spotless. He was reading the paper at the counter and looked up over his reading glasses. "I'm old," he said, slipping them off and into his jacket pocket. "I'm going to take off. Just wanted to say goodbye."

Pam grabbed her purse.

At the front door, he stopped and turned to her. "Thanks for the sleepover and breakfast."

"Thank you," she said. "For breakfast and all your help yesterday. Your family was terrific."

"Our pleasure. Okay, then," he said, leaning down for a soft, chaste kiss.

Pam responded, and the kiss deepened. After a minute, he pulled back. "If we take this any further, you'll definitely be late for Meeting."

She reached up, fingers caressing his cheek. "And we wouldn't want that. Hope you have a great day."

"I'll call you."

She nodded, stepping out into the sunshine, gazing up and down the street. She knew so few of her neighbors, but if she had to guess, at least one of them probably recognized Sandy Rodriguez's truck and knew it had been there all night.

Small towns, she mused as she drove through town, still astounded at the night and morning she'd just spent with one of the village Casanovas.

CHAPTER 16

Sandy had been home about an hour when the doorbell rang. As it was his day with Maisie, he was preparing to head over to the LaSalle estate to pick her up. They'd planned to ride the bike path to Sebring Park and have a picnic. He had packed sandwiches and drinks, and his bike was already in the truck. When he opened the door, he was surprised to see his ex. "Morning. I didn't know you were dropping her off."

"I'm not. She's sick. She's staying home today."

"With?"

"She's at my mom's now."

"This is *my* day, Lolly. We were going to ride bikes, but I can easily stay home and be her nursemaid. We'll veg out and watch movies."

"Not happening," she said, still standing on the doorstep.

"Is this about yesterday and your tantrum directed at Pam Morgan?"

"Fuck you for saying that!" Lolly said. "Don't expect to see Maisie anytime soon either! And don't call." She turned away and stomped off toward her mother's Mercedes.

Sandy followed at her heels. "Lolly, you can't do this."

"Who's gonna stop me?"

"Well let's see, our custody agreement?"

"Give me a break."

"It's also not fair to Maisie or me," he said, keeping his voice low and calm.

"Well, you should have thought of that before you started screwing that whore."

"What the hell is wrong? I've been dating women since we divorced, and you didn't fly off the handle like this."

Lolly turned to face him, eyes blazing. "Maybe I'm just sick of it. You bring me back to this godforsaken town, screw me over, toss me out, and now you're flaunting your whores in front of my misery."

"I'm not sure what you think's going on, but Pam Morgan's certainly not a whore. Besides, we barely know each other."

"Not what I hear."

"What do you want me to say? I like her. She's a friend and a nice person. Since when has that been a crime?"

"Since our daughter and I need to live in this town. Mom's got a wedding, so I've got to go pick her up." She slammed into the car and peeled off.

Sandy looked over at the truck and sighed. "Shit," he said, grabbing his bike and lifting it from the truck.

*****

Richard and Lucy were enjoying a drink on the porch when Mavis LaSalle drove in. He stood and waved. "Hey, gal. To what do we owe this unexpected pleasure? Join us for a drink?"

Tall and stylish, Mavis was dressed casually in flowing linen slacks and a matching top, her dyed black hair wild, violet eyes sparkling with emotion. "White wine would be lovely," she said, hugging each of them, air kisses all around.

When Richard returned with the wine, they all sat. With a curious glance at her husband, Lucy said, "How's the wedding season going?"

"Busy. Just finished a wedding brunch an hour ago."

"Why aren't you home with your feet up?" he asked, smiling kindly.

"I've come about the kids. Your Pam specifically."

"Oh?" he said.

"Did you know she was dating my ex-son-in-law when we were negotiating about the land?"

Richard gave her a sharp look. "No, because I don't think they are. Not that it has any relevance to the property transfer."

"Any relevance? Do you think I would have entered into any business arrangement that involved the man who shattered my daughter's heart?"

Lucy set down her wineglass. "Mavis, this isn't fair and you know it. Lolly was upset yesterday, and she overreacted. As far as we know, Sandy and Pam are friends. If there's more to it, that's their business. Please don't drag Richard into this."

"And listen to you! Her best friend, no less."

"Mavis, I love Lolly and you. You know that, and she does too. I told her I thought she was being unfair to herself and Pam yesterday. They are divorced, and Sandy should be free—as Lolly is—to date anyone he pleases."

"She's right, Mave," Richard said.

Mavis threw up her hands. "Of course she is, but I have to side with my daughter, and she's a wreck."

"But this couldn't be the first woman he's dated?" Richard pointed out.

"No, but this one has hit her hard. Well, I'll leave you to your peace and quiet." Mavis gazed at Lucy. "I'm sure your mom will get after me for rolling in here like gangbusters."

Lucy smiled. "I'm sure she'll understand. And Lolly will be fine."

"I very much doubt that, but time will tell."

"Stay for dinner?" Richard said. "The whole gang'll be here soon."

"Thanks, but it's time to put my feet up."

As Mavis drove away, Richard turned to his wife. "What the hell was that?"

Lucy shook her head. "Not sure, but I fear it's not over."

As they leaned back, Ava, Dan, and the kids drove up the driveway.

"No rest for the weary," she said.

"Wouldn't have it any other way, dear wife of mine." Richard reached over and squeezed her hand.

CHAPTER 17

"Three cheers for the woman of the hour!" Rich said, raising his glass. Sunday dinner was in full swing with Lucy's kids, the Morgan clan—Rich, Ava, Dan and kids, Gail, Weezie, and Pam. Tim was with his family and Harriet, Kyle, and Helen had gone to Lucy's sister Clara's house for the day and evening.

"It was definitely a group effort," Pam said. "But thank you *all*. It was a special day."

By mutual agreement, Lucy and Richard had decided not to mention Mavis's visit until the next morning. Lucy felt strongly that Pam needed to know in case it was ever mentioned, but not tonight. *Tonight was her night!*

The talk was mostly about the garden, but then turned to farm affairs. "Where's Wolfie now?" Ava asked.

"California," Richard said. "I had a few contacts in Napa thanks to Jaybo Dillon. He's headed to Saguaro Valley at the end of the week, lucky duck."

Weezie frowned. "Lucky duck? Dad, where do you come up these expressions?"

"They just come to me, darling. What's happening down at the stables?"

"We've actually booked four lessons. Crackers and Sheba are gonna be busy."

"I invited Gus and Lynn to join us tonight, but they're in Connecticut."

"How's her mom doing?" Gail asked.

"Up and down," Lucy said. "Not great."

"Horrible disease," Richard said. Lynn Casey's mom, Sorcha, had recently been diagnosed with pancreatic cancer, and it was progressing more rapidly than they'd hoped.

"Poor Lynn," Gail saidas Callie served Pam's favorite dessert, floating island.

As they finished dessert and sipped coffee or tea, Pam sat up and cleared her throat, eyes moving around the table. "I know this is coming out of left field, but I think I'm going to step back from my job at the school. I'll still get referrals, and I'm going to do some work for the hospital. I've got a little saved up so I can pay the bills while I build up my private practice. I've applied for a bunch of grants, so I'm hoping the garden will be self-sustaining within six months. This way, I can devote time to it as well."

"Best news I've had this week!" her father said.

"It's not because of what happened," Pam said. "It's more about my wish to put my energies into other things."

"We can always use help at the Lab," Dan said, "but it's messy."

"And we can put you to work here," Richard said.

Pam smiled at her brother-in-law. "I wouldn't be much help there I'm afraid." She turned to her father, then Weezie. "But I am reading up on riding therapy. As you know, I'm not much of a rider, but it interests me."

"I'm sure Maggie Morgan would be a great resource for you," Lucy said.

Pam smiled. "Already have her on speed dial." As the conversation continued, she thought, *Got to keep busy. Anything to keep my mind off Sandy and the relationship that probably should never have begun.*

*****

"It appears that it's just us today," Lucy said to Lynn Monday morning as they sorted boxes of books at Merlin's Closet. Lolly, Lucy's partner, had called to say she couldn't face work or her right now. Lucy wondered at her friend's odd and over-the-top reaction to the relationship between Pam and her ex, but decided to let Lolly cool her heels for a few days.

"Everything okay?" Lynn asked.

"Sort of. My partner can sometimes be moody."

"I heard about what happened Saturday," Lynn said. "Poor Pam."

Lucy gave her a wry smile. "Things will blow over, I'm sure."

The two women worked side by side for the morning. Just before noon, Pam called. She was on her way to the garden, but wanted to catch Lucy before she headed out for lunch. She asked if she had a few minutes to talk, and Lucy agreed to meet her at the garden. "I can use the walk," she said, ringing off. Lucy and Lynn walked out together.

"With Lolly out, you can probably use me for the afternoon, right?" Lynn said.

"Absolutely not!" Lucy said, hugging her. "Baby Sorcha needs you. Nothing is urgent. I'm actually quitting at three to go riding with Richard, so it's a short day. See you in the morning."

After a ten-minute walk, she spied Pam in the back test bed, watering. Avery Coggshall, a local plumber, had installed a simple irrigation system as well as hose ports at various places in the garden. She waved and Pam shut off the water and came to greet her. "Thanks for coming. I'm not taking you away from too much, am I?"

Lucy laughed, eyeing her pretty stepdaughter in jeans and a T-shirt, sleeves rolled up. Farming suited her, even as Lucy noticed dark circles under her eyes. "Happy to get away from the mess. If your father had his way, I'd retire tomorrow."

"Would you want to?"

"Not yet. Maybe in a few years. I'd like to sell it or at least have someone take it over rather than just fold. I owe that to our customers who've stuck with us through the age of Amazon and Walmart."

"Want something to drink? There are still waters and other things in the coolers," Pam asked.

"Water would be lovely."

Pam retrieved two water bottles and handed one to Lucy, sitting down on the bench beside her.

"Thanks," Lucy said. "These benches are great. Where did you get them?"

"Dad ordered them, didn't he tell you? They're from the same company that made the bench at the farm. Mom's bench?"

"Such beautiful workmanship," Lucy said, running her hands over the bench's arm.

"Does it bother you? About the bench at the farm or the garden being named for our mom?" Pam asked.

Lucy reached over and squeezed her hand. "Not at all. It's a lovely tribute to your mother, and that bench at the farm is one of my favorite spots. I often go up and sit in the early morning or late afternoon. Very peaceful. You know I've lived in the village for many years, but never fully appreciated the beauty of the surrounding country until Amy, Rob, and I moved to the farm."

"Do they feel the same?"

Lucy shrugged. "They love the farm, but they miss their home, but fortunately, they can stay there with their dad any time they want." Lucy's ex, Rob Brennan, now lived in their former home that had been in his family for many years.

"Is Amy still going west for the summer?"

Lucy nodded. "She's all signed up to work at Emma's Dream for July. She leaves right after Gail and Tim's wedding."

"Lucky her. I can't wait to go out for Kyle and Harriet's next winter."

"It's a beautiful place," Lucy said.

As they surveyed the neat rows of round-topped beds, a silence fell between them. After several minutes, Pam said, "Dad told me about Mavis's visit."

Lucy gazed over at her with kind eyes. "I thought that might be why you wanted to see me."

"What a mess this has created for you and everybody else. Dad said Lolly refuses to come to work."

Lucy smiled. "She'll get over it. She's my dearest friend, but she's also a hothead."

"But Sandy's been dating women for years. I mean, the man has quite a reputation. Does she do this every time he starts seeing someone?"

"Never. She might make a snide remark, but this is different. Plus she's had a rough time this past year since your dad and I got together. Lolly's lonely. She desperately wants someone in her life."

"Do you think that's it?" Pam asked.

"Truthfully, I don't know. I do have a suspicion, though."

"Oh?"

"I'm not sure I should even say this, but I guess it doesn't hurt as long as you don't take it as gospel. I think Lolly's upset because she sees this relationship as different. Most of the other women Sandy's dated have been groupies, hangers-on, and, frankly, bimbos. It's always pretty clear they aren't going anywhere. Maybe your connection to Richard and me or what she saw when she glimpsed you together seemed different? More serious, maybe?"

"But we hardly know each other!"

"That's true."

"And who's to say I'm not a bimbo?"

"Me, for one. I think your dad and anyone who knows you would also reject the bimbo description."

"So what am I supposed to do?"

"Nothing. It will blow over."

"But in the meantime, your partner refuses to come to work, Mavis LaSalle is furious at me, and Sandy's being denied access to his daughter."

Lucy shook her head. "Oh dear, when did that happen?"

"Yesterday. Sandy called and said he's going to have to take her to court. What a mess!"

Lucy stood up. "I've got a distributor coming at one, but after your dad and I go riding, I'll try to reach Lolly. This is ridiculous."

"Thanks for coming out."

"It's going to be a frequent destination," Lucy said, gazing around. A handful of villagers sat on benches around the property, eating their lunches. "You'll have the whole village here soon."

Pam watched Lucy's departure, then coiled the hose and grabbed her bag. *I know what I have to do, even if it's not going to be easy.*

Chapter 18

Wednesday afternoon after her last client departed, Pam walked the half mile to the garden where she had left her car that morning. She hadn't heard from Sandy and assumed he was embroiled with work and his battle with Lolly over their daughter. *Just as well,* she mused, not relishing the thought of the conversation she knew she needed to have with him.

She had just turned off the hose near the flower bed and was preparing to leave when Sandy's truck pulled into the yard. She paused and waited as he hopped out.

"Hey," he called.

"Hi."

He looked tired and drawn, albeit gorgeous as ever in jeans and an open-collared shirt. She swallowed, strengthening her resolve. All she really wanted was to throw herself into his arms and forget the past few lonely days.

"How's it going?"

"Great so far. You're asking about the garden, right?"

He smiled, sitting on a nearby bench and patting the seat beside him. "Among other things."

Pam came to sit beside him. "Everything's fine. I quit my part-time job at the high school, but they're still referring kids to me. My sister's wedding's coming up, so that keeps us busy. Then there's this." She waved her arms around.

"Pretty amazing. You should be really proud."

"I am. How's things with you? Have you seen Maisie?"

"Nope. My attorney's got a hearing Friday."

"I'm so sorry, Sandy."

"Not your fault." He reached over and took her hand, his fingers massaging her palm. "I'm the one who should be apologizing for throwing you in the middle of this mess. I hope my ex-mother-in-law has backed off."

"You heard about that?"

He shrugged. "Small town. Pam, I came by to see when we can get together."

"I don't think that's a good idea, do you? Especially when you're having to go to court."

"The legal crap has nothing to do with us. My ex is crazy and miserable, and she's decided to take it out on Maisie and me."

Pam sat up, her hand resting on his. "I think this is a bad idea."

"Don't say that."

"Maybe not forever, but for right now." Their eyes met, and Pam glimpsed pain in his.

"I disagree."

"Well, I'm making the decision, then, and I ask that you respect it. I will not be responsible for keeping you from Maisie."

"It'll all get settled Friday."

"Not the anger and hurt. Let's leave things where they are. A lovely memory."

"This is insane!"

"No, this is," Pam said, her hand waving back and forth between them. "I've got to go. I'm meeting someone for dinner. Take care, Sandy."

Pam strode to her car, afraid to look back. As she drove out of the yard, she spied him still sitting on the bench, head in hands.

*****

She didn't have a dinner engagement, but Pam knew what she had to do. After circling through town, she reversed direction and headed out to Mavis LaSalle's estate. Lolly and Maisie lived in the first cottage reached via a dirt drive on the right. Pam had been to the other cottages when shuttling people for her father and Lucy's wedding, but had never been to Lolly's home. As she reached the end of the drive, the small one-story cottage was visible at the back of the one-acre clearing. Like the other two on the property, this one had weathered gray shingles and a shake roof, and a wide porch wrapped around three sides.

Pam parked and headed up the walkway. She had just reached the porch steps when Lolly came out the front door, closing it behind her. "That's far enough. What the hell are you doing here?"

Pam took a deep breath and stood her ground. "Is this where you prefer to talk?"

"I don't want to talk at all, and I sure as hell don't want my daughter involved."

"Fine. I'm here to say that your ex-husband and I are no longer involved, so you can stop punishing him, your daughter, and yourself. You can also stop penalizing your best friend by leaving her short-staffed and worried."

"Are you through?"

"Yes, except to say that I have no idea what I've ever done to you that you hate me as you do, but I'm a big girl. I can take it and have seen worse, but I don't want people I care about to suffer any further with this ridiculous animosity. I'm new in town, and I was looking forward to getting to know you. I'm sorry for Lucy's sake that that doesn't seem likely. I wish you only the best, but please stop this vendetta against your ex-husband. He doesn't deserve it. Take care." Pam turned on her heel and walked quickly to her car. She realized she'd been holding her breath, which she let out with a whoosh. As she started the car and turned to go, she saw a shadow at the cottage window, dark curls ringing a round little face. *Poor baby*, she thought as she drove away.

CHAPTER 19

The days and weeks following the garden opening were busy ones for Pam and her crew of volunteers. A number of villagers had signed up the day of the groundbreaking to volunteer at the garden, and Pam had to meet with them to go over equipment and responsibilities. She tried to be on site as much as possible and to check in throughout each day. Glad of the busyness that kept her mind occupied, her heart was sad in the downtimes. Those brief but precious moments she had shared with Sandy Rodriguez. Their lovemaking had been transformative, but it was the quiet, companionable moments she missed most.

There was also Gail's upcoming wedding. Pam was her maid of honor and had a million little duties associated with that. To add to the days, word of her practice had reached surrounding towns and she had a growing patient list, mostly adolescents, but also a few regular adults. She and Elise enjoyed working together and were negotiating a move to larger quarters with two consulting rooms so they could both be there together. For a variety of reasons, Pam preferred this, not the least of which was safety.

A third of the garden plots had already been adopted by villagers, and Pam was in the midst of an orientation to a new plot for a young family, when Raffi Rodriguez strolled through the arbor, looking like a million bucks in a suit that had to have cost more than three months of her salary. She left the Flanderses to begin their work, and came to say hello.

"Hi," she said. "Are you here to volunteer?"

He gave her a hundred-watt smile that no doubt left a trail of broken hearts from here to Bayport. "I'd be happy to sign up, but not today."

"Can I help you with something, or are you just looking around?"

"I actually came to see you. Got a minute?"

Surprised, Pam said, "Of course." She walked to a nearby bench and sat down. After a glance at the bench to make sure it was clear of debris, he sat beside her.

"It's about my brother."

"Oh no, is something wrong? I heard the court thing went away and he's been seeing Maisie regularly again."

"It did and he is. That's not why I'm here. He'll never say it, but the guy's in agony. He misses you like I've never seen him miss a woman before."

She met his eyes, the same dark eyes as his brother's, but with a sharpness that Sandy's didn't have. *Cunning? Determination?* "I'm sure that's an exaggeration."

"Maybe, but he's a hurting cowboy. Can't you give him a break?"

"It's not that simple."

"The court case got thrown out."

"Good," she said.

"So it's not an issue."

"Good, because I assured Lolly LaSalle that I would not be seeing him anymore."

"That's bullshit."

"Maybe, but I gave my word, and I will not be responsible for keeping a child from her father."

"Even if you're in love with that father?"

She looked him in the eyes again. "Even then."

Raffi stood up. "Well, I'll let you get back to it." He pulled a business card from his jacket pocket and handed it to her. "Feel free to sign me up for time on Saturdays or Sundays, and I'll put it on my calendar."

Confused, she gazed up at him. "Excuse me?"

"Volunteering? Here in the garden."

"Oh yes, thanks. That'd be great."

As he disappeared through the arbor, she shook her head. *Could life get any stranger? Maybe Aunt Celia's right— there's blissful anonymity in the big city!*

CHAPTER 20

The week of Gail's wedding was a blur of activity. Wolfie returned from his West Coast winery tour on Spark Foster's private jet along with his father's brother, and his wife. Uncle Ben and Aunt Leonora were accompanied by Spark, their lifelong friend, who took advantage of any opportunity to visit with Lucy's mother, Helen Winthrop. The two had become good friends on Helen's trips to Saguaro Valley. It was the Valley's busiest season, so only Ben, Leonora, and Spark had made the trip. To make up for their absence now, the entire Morgan clan was planning a party celebrating Gail and Tim in Saguaro Valley during "Wedding Week" in December.

The elder Morgans were staying at the farm and Spark with Helen. Spark had hired a car and driver to shuttle the group from the airport to the village. Thursday morning, Gail, Pam, and Weezie waited at the farm to greet everyone and help get them settled in. None of the travelers had arrived when Tim drove in at noon to say hello and take Gail to lunch. They still had a few things to work out, and between the demands of two families, they had barely had a minute to themselves.

"Go," Pam said. "We can certainly handle the cousins. You two are much more important!"

After parking in town, Tim gazed over at her. "So are you sure you're ready to marry an old man like me?"

Gail reached over and squeezed his arm. "Surer than I've been of anything in my life. And I can't wait till Sunday when I'll have you all to myself for a whole week!"

His eyes softened as he gazed into hers. "Me too, baby. Me too."

They grabbed takeout at the Café and decided to eat in the garden. "It's become the hot spot for lunch," he told her as they found a bench in the shade.

"It's beautiful, isn't it? Look how many beds are already taken. Let's get one. Want to?"

He grinned, reaching over to tuck a lock of her auburn hair behind her ear. "With all your land and my family's?"

"But this would be ours until we get our own place. I mean, we wouldn't take it if someone else wanted it, but would you mind if I asked Pam?"

Ruth Penny, one of the garden volunteers, strolled by and tipped her broad straw hat at them. Tim waved at Ruth, then said, "When have I ever denied you anything, baby?"

"It will be really cool! We can plant flowers and herbs and maybe a few tomatoes?"

"Anything you like. Although I'm pretty fond of cilantro. Can you throw some of that in?"

"Absolutely! I'll ask Pam this afternoon, and we can start planting right after the honeymoon. Honeymoon," she said, her eyes dreamy. "That has such a lovely sound."

"Speaking of Pam, do you think it's going to be a problem that he's at the wedding?"

"No, she's a big girl."

"Does she know?"

Gail smiled at him. "Not exactly."

"What does that mean? Don't you think you should tell her?"

"I will, but she's been so down and stressed these past few weeks, I didn't want to add to it."

"I couldn't not have him after all he's done for me."

"I know, and Dad understands. He really likes Sandy."

"Well, no surprises and no blowups on wedding day, baby. Tell Pam. The Rodríguezes are like a second family to me."

"No worries." She leaned forward for a kiss.

"No secluded spot around this garden for a nooner, is there?"

His mischievous grin always melted Gail's heart and made her want to jump him on the spot. "Believe me, if there was, I'd have dragged you there. I've missed you so much."

*****

Later that afternoon, the bustle of arrivals over, Pam and Gail were sipping iced tea on the porch. Ben, Leonora, and their father had gone for a drive, and they planned to meet Lucy for a drink at the garden. "Are you going over there to show 'em around?" Gail asked.

"No, let Dad do it. It's as much his as mine, and he's really proud of it."

"Sis, there's something I wanted to discuss with you. I know it's been busy and you haven't been involved in invitations, wedding lists, and so forth."

"No, I'm sorry," Pam said. "But as your maid of honor, I'm here for you now. Two hundred percent."

"I know you are. That's not it. I just… I just didn't know if you knew about the close relationship of the Miller and Rodriguez families? Rosa is Faith Miller's best friend, so the entire family is invited."

"Of course they are," Pam said. "I know that. No worries at all."

Gail grinned. "Big sigh of relief. Because I don't want you to feel uncomfortable."

"I'll be fine. Breaking it off with Sandy was my decision, and I did it for the right reasons."

"But you haven't seen him in three weeks. Is that going to be tough for you?"

Pam set down her tea and looked at her sister. "I guess we'll find out, but I'm thinking it will be fine. It has to be. This is *your day*."

Gail smiled, leaning back and closing her eyes. "Thanks, sis. Now let's enjoy these last few minutes of peace and quiet we'll have for the next three days!"

CHAPTER 21

Thursday evening, the Morgans hosted an informal dinner at the farm. With Dennis Farrell's help, Callie had the grills going with chicken, hamburgers, and hot dogs. Family—Millers and Morgans—friends, and out-of-town guests were invited to drop in. People came and went all evening as Richard and his brother and Leonora held court on the back terrace. Fortunately, it was a clear, balmy night, so they didn't need the barn, which was already set up for Saturday's reception.

"What a night!" Spark said as he chatted with Helen Winthrop, Ben and Leonora Morgan, and Richard and Lucy. The younger generation had congregated on the lawn below. Ben and Teddy, Gail's brothers, had arrived that morning and were entertaining their niece and nephew, Sasha and Cameron, along with Gus and Lynn's older two kids. Frisbees, soccer balls, and other lawn toys flew through the air. Weezie joined in when not helping with the grill.

"Aren't we lucky with our kids?" Ben Senior said. "Nothing more fun than watchin' them play. In fact, I'm tempted to join in."

"But you will not," Leonora said.

Tim and Gail chatted with her siblings and some of their friends in the shade of an enormous maple tree. As Dan Fielding, Ava's husband, stood up and tossed a frisbee back into the fray, he turned to Tim. "What'll we do next week? Poachers'll have a field day with you gone."

"Well, you could grab Brick to help out," Tim said, referring to his younger brother. "I trust him with the boat. He's pulling pots for me."

"I'm on it," Dan said. "Is he around tonight?"

"He was, but he left. Mom's got everyone over there working overtime to get ready for tomorrow night."

"Is there anything we can do?" Pam asked. "Between Dad and Salters, Saturday's pretty well organized."

"Thanks, but we're good," Tim said. "It seems kinda quiet here without the Arizona contingent."

"Oh, you'll have a week of them next winter," Wolfie said. "They've got more shit planned than you can imagine. Those people really know how to party."

"That's right, you were just out there, right?" Tim asked.

Wolfie nodded. "And I didn't stop for four days."

"When do you go out, Amy?" Ava asked Lucy's daughter, who'd been quietly listening to the conversation with two of her friends.

"I'm flying back on Mr. Foster's jet," she said.

"Lucky you!" Ava said. "Where are you staying out there?"

"I'll mostly be at the camp. I'm a counselor, so I'll have a cabin of kids. But when I'm not at camp, I'll be staying with Maggie and Ben Morgan."

"Wait'll you see their house," Wolfie said. "One of the most incredible spots in the world."

"And, I get my own golf cart to drive around," Amy said. "I'm so excited."

Pam listened to the conversation but said little. It seemed as if everyone had exciting plans except her. There was the garden, of course, and she was thrilled with how it was shaping up. It would be fun to have Tim and Gail take one of the beds. She had high hopes that all would be taken by the end of the month. Despite the garden and her growing therapy practice, she was sad and lonely. *There. I've admitted it. I'm lonely because I miss him.*

*****

For a Thursday night, the club was hopping. One of the most popular local bands, the Funky White Hombres, was playing, so the crowd was local and raucous. Sandy and Murph stood behind one of the three bars, observing the dance floor as six bartenders and eight waitresses rushed to keep up with the crowd. "We may want to hire extra help the next time the Hombres play," Sandy said. "It's a Saturday in July, right?"

"Yup," Murph said. "We'll need people out on the decks."

"You sure you're okay about Saturday night? Jimmy Rae draws a crowd too."

"Got it, boss. By the way, the blonde at table seven's been asking for you."

"Good for her. You know her?"

"Nope. Not a local, but she came with the high school crowd," Murph said.

"Yet another reason to stay away from her."

"When has that stopped you?"

"Since I got old," Sandy said.

"And fell in love with Pam Morgan."

"Leave it, Murph."

"I can leave it, but can you?"

"The woman made it very clear that she wants nothing to do with me."

"As I've said before—when has that stopped you? Come on, man, you've been moping around here for weeks. Maisie's back on your regular schedule, and your ex has calmed down. Time to get back in the saddle."

"Skip the cowboy metaphors and go check on the kegs. The north bar has gotta be ready for another couple."

"Will do," Murph said, leaving him.

His manager was right, of course. He was in love with Pam. Much as he tried to push it away or tamp it down, he couldn't deny it. The thought of another woman left him cold, and all he could think about was her smooth, peach skin, her lovely blue eyes, soft and warm as she gazed at him. It would be a tough Saturday, but the Millers were good friends. He'd get through it.

CHAPTER 22

Friday night went by with a blur of Millers and Morgans. Raffi, Sonia, and Milly Rodriguez came with their mother, while their father, Cesar, stayed at the restaurant to hold down the fort. Raffi spied Pam standing with her four brothers on his way in and said, "If you're wondering, he's at the Club."

As the group passed by, Wolfie turned to her. "What was that about?"

"Don't ask," Pam said, excusing herself to find her fellow bridesmaids. They were planning a little toast and song after dinner, and they needed to rehearse.

"How you doing, sis?" Gail asked, having also noticed the encounter with Raffi.

Weezie feigned a swoon. "Raffi Rodriguez is the most gorgeous man alive. Think I have a chance with him?"

Pam and Ava exchanged looks before Ava said, "He's rarely around. He travels all the time, according to Grace." Rosa's friend and Tim's aunt, Grace Childs Straley ran the Lab where Dan and Ava worked and where Tim collaborated on the Horseshoe Crab rescue project.

"I love travel," Weezie said. "Are we done with our skit?"

"No," Pam said. "We haven't even started."

"Well, let's hurry up so I can go talk to Raffi!"

Pam rolled her eyes, then looked at Ava. "Doesn't Gail look happy?"

Ava nodded. "Sure does. Tim's a great guy, and he's over-the-moon happy too. It's about time."

They practiced in the Miller's side yard until the dinner call came. "We're ready," Ava said. "Pam will start us off with the toast, then we'll chime in."

"Later!" Weezie said, running off in the direction of a group that included Raffi.

"Is she ever going to learn that subtle may be more effective?" Pam said.

Her sister laughed. "Weezie? No way. From what I've heard about her clone, cousin Ruthie Morgan has gotten pretty far with that same ridiculous personality, so you never know."

As they headed for the tables, Ben and Leonora Morgan caught up with them. "Hi, darlins," she said.

Blonde hair beautifully coiffed, Leonora was dressed in stylish denim capris and a white embroidered jersey. Her tall handsome husband's arm was draped on her shoulder. *The silver foxes*, the cousins called Ben Morgan and Spark Foster.

"Hey, gals! Where are your beaus?" Ben asked.

"I just said hi to your handsome husband," she said to Ava, "but where's your guy, honey? Pretty girl like you needs a guy."

Pam smiled. "Sorry, Aunt Nora. No guy, but not for lack of trying. Now let's find you a towel or a bib to protect that cute white top."

"Honey, I come from barbecue country," Leonora said, pulling an enormous terrycloth bib from her purse. "I'm always prepared."

Her husband's arm circled her shoulders as he gazed down with affection. "That she is. You check in at the end of the evening. If there's a spot on her, I'll eat my hat."

The sisters laughed as the group made its way to the buffet line. "This is my kind of party," Spark Foster said, arm around Helen Winthrop as they joined their good friends.

Halfway through dinner the toasts began. Coop Merrick, Tim's best man offered the first one, a somewhat raucous salute to the end of his friend's bachelorhood. He ended by turning to Gail. "Tim Miller is a lucky man, Gail Morgan. You're the best thing that's ever happened to him. You're kind, brave, and strong, not to mention beautiful. I'd be insanely jealous of my buddy if I weren't so damn happy for him. May you both have long, happy lives together and be even happier than you are at this moment in the years to come." When Coop raised his glass, tears sparkled in his eyes.

Then it was Pam's turn. She stood on shaky legs, unfolding her speech. "I wish I could speak as eloquently or spontaneously as Coop about this incredible couple, but I took a few notes. From the moment Tim came into Gail's life, there was a light in her that I'd never seen before. It was the promise of a beautiful dream on which she never gave up. I have never seen her so happy and know that Tim put the sparkle in her eye and joy in her heart that continue to grow and blossom—excuse the mixed metaphors. My sisters and I would like to offer a small ditty that expresses our love for Gail and our joy for these two."

The three sisters launched into the song they had created for Gail and Tim set to the tune of "Michael Row Your Boat Ashore. "Pam met Sandy's eyes in the crowd and was momentarily thrown by the intensity of feeling she glimpsed there. Shaking herself, she linked arms with Weezie and Ava, turning her attention to Gail. As the last lines of "Timothy, Row Your Boat Ashore" trailed off, she smiled. *I'm okay. Surrounded by people I love and who love me, I'll always be okay.*

The crowd applauded, and the sisters found their seats again. Richard Morgan and Rex Miller both offered toasts, then Ben Morgan Senior stood and congratulated the couple, ending his words with, "Every time we come east, it gets better and better. Now we have a whole new family to invite to Saguaro Valley. I hope the Millers, friends, and family will come west so Leonora, Spark, and I can repay your kindness and welcome you to our homes. There are plenty of homes and plenty of room, so *all* are invited anytime."

As the evening wore down, people milled about, and Pam ran into Raffi. "Hey, nice job on the toast and song," he said.

"Thanks."

"Only sorry my brother couldn't have heard you."

As it was clear he'd had a lot to drink, Pam gazed around for a graceful exit. She took several steps backward. "Would you excuse me? I've got to find my ride."

His gorgeous dark eyes blazed with passion and something else. *Anger? Resentment?* "I'm not giving up on you two." He moved closer, and Pam could smell the scotch on his breath. "Raffi, I don't know what to say to you."

"There's my pretty niece," Ben Morgan said, draping an arm around Pam's shoulders. "Can an old man escort you to your car?"

"I thought you'd never ask," she said, smiling at her uncle and nodding to Raffi.

As they strolled off arm in arm, Ben whispered, "Hope I wasn't interrupting, honey. Looked like you needed rescuing."

She leaned against his strong shoulder. "My hero. How did it take our families so long to get together?"

"Don't know, but now that it's happened, there'll be no pullin' us apart." As they neared the group going back to the farmhouse, he kissed the top of her head. "Night, darlin'."

"Night, Uncle Ben."

As Pam headed off to find Rich, who had driven her to the dinner, she smiled, already in love with her uncle, aunt, and cousins. She couldn't wait to get to Saguaro Valley for Kyle and Harriet's wedding. *Now I just have to get through tomorrow and seeing Sandy, then I can relax and get on with my life.*

*****

Closing time at the club, Sandy was barking orders to anyone in earshot. "What the hell's wrong with him?" Gary, one of the bartenders said as Murph passed by.

Lois, a waitress set a tray of empty glasses on the bar. "Want my opinion?"

Not especially, but I'm sure we're gonna get it, Murph thought.

"Woman trouble. That's my guess."

Murph found Sandy in the kitchen laying into one of the dishwashers. "Hey, boss, why don't you head on home and I'll close?"

Sandy turned to him, eyes blazing. "Do I look like I'm ready to head on home?"

"Not sure, but you're sure acting like an asshole," Murph said under his breath.

"You bucking to get fired?"

"Go ahead, fire my ass. See if I care. No one should have to take this crap, especially from you."

"Fine, you're fired. Get the hell out. Now!"

Incredulous, Murph stared at him for about thirty seconds, then said, "Okay, fine," and stalked out of the kitchen, slamming the back door.

"That worked out well, didn't it?" Sandy said to the dishwasher, Eddie, who was pretending to be invisible. Not waiting for an answer, he stomped out of the room and found Gary.

"Hey, Gary, do you mind locking up tonight?"

"What about Murph?" Gary asked.

"History," Sandy said as he grabbed his jacket and headed out.

CHAPTER 23

When Sandy woke with a terrible headache, he remembered the reason why. He'd drunk too much, acted like a complete ass, and fired his best friend. *Christ, what must Murph think of me? Lolly's right, I'm unfit to be a dad.* He made coffee and sat on the deck, bare-chested in pajama bottoms, and pondered the day ahead. The Millers were the closest thing to cousins he had, and there was no way he could blow off the wedding, but the thought of seeing Pam hurt. He was immune to Lolly and her slights and jabs, but catching a glimpse of the woman he adored was going to hurt. Bad.

First Murph, then the wedding. He showered and took three Advils. Thirty minutes later, the world was looking marginally better, which wasn't saying much. He pulled on jeans and a tee, deciding it was a flip-flop morning. Murph lived in a duplex at the far end of town on the road to Southport. When Sandy parked the truck, he spied Murph in the side yard, cutting the grass. When he saw his boss, he paused, then turned away, resuming his mowing.

Sandy watched him go back and forth a few times, then approached, grabbing his shoulder. "Hey, man, can we talk?"

Murph shrugged out of his grasp and killed the engine. Hands on hips, he said, "What?"

"I'm sorry. I was a world-class shit. And you're right, I've been acting like a horse's ass for weeks now. You guys don't deserve it."

"Got that right."

"Can we forget last night?"

"What's that mean?"

"Would you consider coming back to work? There's a raise in it."

Murph grinned. "This 'cause you need me to take over tonight?"

"No, it's because I can't do the club without you and because you're my best friend."

Murph's caramel-brown eyes glinted with mischief. "Yeah, I'll come back on one condition."

"Anything, buddy."

"Save us all the crap and call that therapist of yours. Get an appointment ASAP."

Sandy smiled, opening his arms and hugging the man he considered a brother. "Deal. I really am sorry, man."

"I know you are, boss. Once you get your head out of your ass, you'll be fine."

"Ha-ha. Gotta go. I've gotta see a lady about a head that needs shrinking."

"Today?"

"Already called her before I headed over here."

"But how'd you—?"

"You forget, I dated the fair Elise when she first moved to town."

"Isn't that a conflict of interest?"

"She saved my life when I was picking up the pieces from Lolly."

"Hmm…a man of hidden depths."

"You bet your sweet ass. I'll check in tonight either by phone, or I'll stop by after the wedding.

*****

"What a wonderful cook your Callie is," Leonora said as she helped herself to more coffee from the buffet. Callie had set out several breakfast casseroles as well as mountains of bacon, ham, and sausage. There were also flaky croissants, a variety of muffins, and several kinds of quick breads. "This lemon bread is to die for! I wonder if she'd give me the recipe to take back to Carmela, our cook?"

"I'll make you a copy and slip it in your room," Callie said as she set out a fresh pitcher of orange juice. Amy and Rob, Lucy's teenagers, had already eaten and were off for a few hours with friends.

"Can't wait to get you girls out to the Valley," Ben Senior said to Lucy.

Lucy smiled. "She's so excited, but also, Amy's feeling the pangs of the summer without all her buddies."

"She'll meet new ones out there. Our counselors are a great group. Some real cute ones too," Leonora said, winking.

As Richard and Lucy sat with his brother and Leonora, the long table slowly filled with Morgans—Teddy, Ben, Wolfie, Pam, and Weezie wandered in followed by the bride-to-be. White as a sheet, Gail served herself a tiny dollop of casserole and a slice of blueberry bread. The others exchanged glances as she sat at the far end of the table, staring into space.

"You feelin' okay, princess?" Richard asked.

Pam set a mug of steaming coffee beside her sister. "Drink this. It'll perk you up."

"I don't need perking up. I need a lobotomy. I can't do this! I can't get married in front of a bunch of people."

"You're a PR person, for goodness' sakes," Weezie said. "It's your job to be around people."

"Behind the scenes, not front and center. I can't do it. I'm going to call Tim and say we can have the party and get married by ourselves at the courthouse."

"In front of a bunch of strangers?" Pam said. "As your maid of honor, I'm telling you…no, I'm ordering you to pull yourself together!"

"Leave her alone, honey," Richard said, gazing over at Lucy and Leonora.

Leonora popped up and came to sit beside Gail. "This is wedding jitters, pure and simple. Why, when I was gettin' ready to marry my handsome guy, they had to give me smelling salts, then a healthy shot of brandy. Even then, my maid of honor, Patsy Foster, had to slap me across the face, then stuff me into my dress. But once I caught sight of my groom waitin' for me in that church, I was just fine."

Hanging on her aunt's every word, Gail sipped her coffee. "And no one could tell?"

"Not a soul. Now you just buck up, let your family help you, and you'll be ready to walk down and meet that gorgeous guy of yours this afternoon. I guarantee it."

Miraculously, her aunt's talk put some color in Gail's face. Later, as she and her siblings scattered, the elder Morgans sat chatting with Richard and Lucy over a last cup of coffee. Richard gazed over at Leonora. "So I can't imagine you as a jittery bride."

As her husband rolled his eyes, Leonora winked. "Some of it was true. I was in heaven when I spied my honey waiting for me."

"The rest is pure fiction," Ben said. "She was behind the scenes directing things like a general."

Leonora patted his arm, smiling at their hosts. "A little white lie won't hurt if it helps your baby relax. What a pretty little thing she is, and she doesn't even know it."

"Thanks, Nora. We owe you big-time," Richard said.

"No, you don't. Now, what needs to be done around here? I love a good project!"

*****

"So it's been a while," Elise Nolan said, ushering Sandy into the consulting room. "I was surprised to hear from you."

"You okay with this?"

"Would I have said yes if it wasn't?"

The lithe, dark-haired therapist curled herself into one of the overstuffed armchairs, inviting him to sit. "Oh, I'm sorry, can I get you anything? Water?"

"I'm fine. You look good, Elise. How have you been?"

"Great, thanks, but we're here to talk about you."

"You're right, of course. It's about a woman."

"Yes?"

"Can I give you some background?"

She smiled, waving her arm in encouragement. "Your time."

He described the past month and his relationship, or lack of, with Pam. When he ended, she said, "How can I help?"

"Tell me what to do. I really need you to tell me."

"First, I want to say that we're on delicate ground. Pam is now my colleague and friend."

"Please, Elise. I'm desperate here. I promise if I need more therapy, I'll drive to Bayport."

She smiled. "Okay, but just this once. I have to start by saying—to use a very unprofessional, inappropriate expression—so the mighty oak has fallen."

"Guess I deserved that after our history."

"Ancient history. Let's concentrate on the present, shall we? You're in love with Pam Morgan, aren't you?"

"Yup."

"Are you sure?"

"Yup."

"Then tell her."

"It won't matter. She won't come between Maisie and me."

"Relationships are messy. I don't have to tell you that."

"Nope."

"Give it time. Don't rush it."

"Thanks, Elise. I didn't deserve this, but I'm grateful."

"You should be. Now get out of here. And come see me again if you need to."

"Will do. You got a guy in your life?"

"None of your business. Now, scoot."

CHAPTER 24

On a perfect June afternoon, a smiling Gail Morgan, resplendent in an off-white muslin dress and a ring of flowers in her hair, clutched her father's hand as she walked through the barn past the assembled guests to meet Tim Miller, handsome and calm in his gray linen suit. After a kiss from her dad, she took Tim's hand and sighed. She'd made it. She hadn't tripped and fallen, and she was holding the hand of the man she loved more than life itself.

"You look amazing," Tim whispered, bending to kiss her forehead. "You ready?"

She nodded, and they turned to face the pastor. Anna Goodspeed, the pastor of the small UCC church in town where the Millers worshipped. Anna smiled at them, then leaned closer. "He's right. You look gorgeous."

Pam stood with bridesmaids Karen and Rachel Miller, Tim's sisters, and Ava and Weezie. Cameron, the ring bearer, surrendered the rings to Coop, and he and Sasha, the flower girl, their jobs completed, skipped over to sit with their father.

Pam smiled at her sister, so happy for her. Like the bride, the bridesmaids would be shedding their dresses for jeans soon after the ceremony, so Gail had insisted on simple and inexpensive. She had chosen the color, a pale peach, and let the bridesmaids choose from a variety of styles. Pam had selected one she knew flattered her slender frame and that she would wear again. Sleek and simple, it was sleeveless, with a scoop neck, a racer back, and a mid-length style that draped her body perfectly, accentuating every subtle curve. The bridesmaids also had flowers in their hair and wore simple silver jewelry.

The moment Sandy caught sight of her, his body reacted, his erection straining his jeans. This was going to be a big problem if he didn't settle down. He couldn't take his eyes off her. So beautiful and delicate, her pale peach skin was almost the same color as her dress. And that dress—way too sexy and hot for a clambake. Thank God she'd be changing afterward, or he'd have to borrow an apron from the Salters crew to wear for the evening. Geez, the woman turned him on in a way that was almost scary. He was usually the one in charge, not the other way round. *Get a grip, man*, he thought as he watched her sweet ass swish down the aisle.

Gail and Tim exchanged traditional vows, and the short ceremony ended with Tim sweeping her into his arms for a long kiss as applause rang through the barn. Afterward, there was a receiving line on the grass outside. After guests greeted the couple and wedding party, they began mingling for a long, languid cocktail hour.

Pam was chatting with Lynn Casey when she caught sight of Sandy two people behind the Caseys in the line. Her heart stopped as she spied him chatting with Gail and Tim in the easy way he had. *Oh my goodness*, did he look hot in jeans and an open-collared gray Irish linen sport shirt. She gulped, wondering how she'd get through a hug from that!

"You okay?" Lynn said, "You look a little pale."

She smiled. "Fine. It's been a crazy few days."

Lynn moved on, and Gus hugged her. "Great job. You all look beautiful."

Finally, there he was, standing in front of her, smiling that amazing smile that never failed to send fire from her toes to the top of her head, his dark eyes arresting. "Hello," she managed to sputter as he came forward to wrap her in a strong embrace that lingered a bit longer than propriety allowed.

As he stepped back, he whispered, "There should be a law about you in that dress."

Pam blushed crimson, whispering back. "Well, I'll be removing it soon!"

"That sounds even better," he said, as his brothers edged up behind him, eager to greet her, then get a drink.

"Better move along, Mr. Rodriguez," she said, not daring to meet those coal-black eyes again. The thought of removing her dress in his presence was enough to send her knees knocking.

Raffi and his brothers offered congratulations with grins that revealed their amusement at the scene they'd just witnessed. Pam straightened her back and gave herself a pep talk. *You can do this. Only a few more minutes.*

"Hey, Ms. Morgan," Vincent Rodriguez said. "Great dress. Looks like it was made for you."

Pam knew Vincent only slightly from seeing him at the Grille where he bartended. Unlike Raffi, his expression was more open and genuine . She smiled and thanked him as the family continued to pass by and offer their congratulations.

After formal photos, the wedding party retired to the house to change into casual clothes. There was a band coming later, but Gail and Tim were very happy to dance in jeans and sneakers, so there was no formal first dance in their wedding attire. While she felt safer and more comfortable in jeans, Pam hated to slip out of the dress she knew had had such an effect on Sandy Rodriguez. As she hung up the peach sheath, she thought back to the receiving line and the way Lolly LaSalle had skirted around her after greeting the bride and groom. *No matter.* There were enough people around that she could avoid Sandy's angry ex-wife. The truth was she didn't blame Lolly one bit for her feelings. Infidelity was unforgivable.

As she and Weezie stepped out of the house and into the cocktail party, they ran into Helen, Lucy's mom, who was chatting with Faith Miller and Frankie Brown, two of the infamous Darn Yarners. Every member of the group was invited, but only Belle Pollart, who with her husband, Will, ran the docks and fishery, was unable to make it. For the first time in twenty-five years, the Pollarts had left their employees in charge and had taken a long-planned trip to Jamaica.

"Hey, ladies," Weezie called. "Let's get this party started!"

"Already in high gear from my vantage point," Frankie said, pointing to the wide grassy area at the side of the barn where their brothers Wolfie and Teddy were chasing Cameron, Sasha, and toddler Laura along with Dulcie and Cal Casey. The squeals of the children's laughter was infectious, and before they knew it, Weezie took off to join them.

Pam smiled at Helen. "At least my sister's predictable."

"She's a sweetheart," Helen said as Spark Foster approached and handed her a glass of white wine.

"Why, hello, darlin'! You were sure a knockout comin' down the aisle, not that you aren't now. Boy oh boy, wait'll the valley cowboys see you next winter."

She smiled. "Thanks, Spark. I feel more like myself in these jeans, but it is fun to dress up."

"'Course it is, 'specially a pretty gal like yourself. Can I get you something to drink?"

"Thanks, but I'll get something in a bit. You enjoy yourself." Pam wandered across the grass, wondering if she'd remembered all her maid of honor duties. She was pretty sure she was free until it was time for Gail and Tim to leave. She had promised her sister she'd help with last-minute goodbyes. The couple was staying the night at the Oceanside, a small, historic inn to the south of the village. After tomorrow's wedding brunch, the couple was driving to Maine for a week at Arcadia. Richard had pulled some strings and gotten them one of the premier cabins in the national park. They would spend most of their time in Arcadia, but Gail also wanted to spend a night in Portland on the way home so she could show him the farm and some of the special places of their childhood.

Lost in thought, she was startled when she literally ran into Sandy. His strong muscular chest pressed against her, driving the breath from her body in a whoosh! "Oh!" she said.

"Whoa." He grasped her arms to steady her.

Flustered, Pam pressed her hands against his chest, steadying herself. "Sorry… thinking about my wedding duties."

"No apology necessary." He held her, gazing down with warmth and something more. "But if you stay pressed against me much longer, I'm gonna need to grab a napkin from one of those pretty tables."

"It'll take more than a napkin to cover that!" she said, feeling his erection surge against her jeans. Then, shocked at her bold words, she stepped back.

Grinning, Sandy regarded her, every inch of her sending him into overdrive. He shifted, subtly adjusting himself as he fought for control. "I miss the dress."

"Hardly appropriate for a clambake."

"Still, would have been fun to slip you out of it."

Blushing, Pam looked around to see if anyone was listening. Fortunately, they were on their own, a good distance from most of the wedding guests. "Is this how it's going to be every time I run into you?"

He nodded. "Pretty much. Until you consent to go out with me again."

God, the man is perfect! Every inch of her screamed *I want you!* Not just his body. There was something soulful and deep about Sandy Rodriguez. It was as if he got her and knew what she needed more than anyone else in her life. Pam shook herself. *Maybe he hasn't got a clue about me, just lots of practice pleasing women to get what he wants.* "Well, that's not going to happen, so you better take a lot of cold showers."

As she turned away, he grasped her arm. "What's happened to you? This isn't the Pam Morgan I know talking."

Pam shook her head, but stayed silent.

"Please Pam, I'm dying here."

"I can't. I will not come between you and Maisie, and that's that. You're right, the sassy talk isn't me, but I'm trying to cope the best way I can. Please let go." For an instant, she met his eyes and saw sadness reflected in their depths. "I'm sorry, Sandy, but it's for the best. This is a really small town, as you keep reminding me."

"Okay, I'll let go on one condition."

"What's that?"

"That you dance with me tonight. One dance, then I'll leave you alone."

Pam knew she should refuse. It would be sweet torture having his arms around her knowing that it was only for three minutes. "Okay, one dance."

Sandy smiled and let her go. "I'll find you, babe."

CHAPTER 25

Sated on clams, lobster, and all the trimmings, guests drifted from the tables to sample a variety of ice-cream treats Salters had placed on two buffets. The bar was still open, and coffee and tea had been set out. Tim sat with his arm draped around Gail, surveying the crowd and smiling. "You look like a pig in shit, husband of mine."

"And I feel like one. I've got everything I need right here." He grabbed her hand, bringing it to his lips, kissing each knuckle. "I love you, babe. Only thing that'll make me happier than this is getting you out of those jeans at the Oceanside tonight."

She turned and kissed him. "Mmm… Something to look forward to. For the record, I'm happy too. Happier than I ever thought possible."

Tim grinned. "Nosy as they are, we're damn lucky with our families, aren't we?"

"Sure are." She gazed across the barn. "And speaking of our families, it looks like another Miller-Morgan friendship may be developing."

Tim followed her gaze and spied his sister Karen talking and laughing with Rich Morgan. "He better watch out with her. I love my sister, but she's the worst love-'em-and-leave-'em in our family."

"No way!"

"Yup. Karen's been engaged about a gazillion times, but always finds an excuse to break it off. Think runaway bride."

"I never knew that," Gail said, her mouth curled up in the cute expression of surprise he adored.

"Gotta kiss you, babe," he said, capturing her lips, drawing her away from her observation of Rich and Karen.

When she finally came up for air, Gail caught her father watching them from across the room. Richard gave her a thumbs-up. *Yikes! We'd better save it for the Oceanside*, she thought, turning to Tim. "Well, Rich isn't a love 'em-and-leave-'em guy. He's more the 'bait, hook, drift' type."

Tim laughed. "Ah-ha! Fishing metaphors, something this country bumpkin can understand!"

"Bumpkin indeed, says the Dartmouth and Wesleyan grad." She leaned against his strong chest and sighed. "I am *sooo* glad I don't have to date anymore."

Tim kissed the top of her head. "I certainly hope not!"

*****

"I can't believe we've lived here almost a year and not run into each other," Rich said, thinking the short, compact little brunette with those lapis-blue eyes was hard to miss. "It's been great talking to you,"

Karen smiled at the eldest Morgan son, his piercing green eyes and runner's build more than interesting. He had a nervous habit of brushing errant strands of brown hair from his forehead as he began to speak that she found incredibly sexy. "I've caught glimpses of you. I have a part-time job that brings me to town, but the rest if the time, I'm at the farm. If I socialize, it's with Harriet and Kyle. Poor Kyle, he must get so sick of me grabbing her for adventures."

"I don't know. My cousin's pretty easygoing. I'm sure he's happy you guys are out having fun."

"We are so incredibly lucky to have him here. When we lost our large animal vet last year, we were really stuck. There's beginning to be a shortage of vets nowadays, particularly ones who treat large animals."

"Why's that, with so many animal lovers in the world?" he asked, noticing the saucy turn of her lips as she smiled.

"Kyle says it's cause veterinary school is so incredibly expensive. Just like med school. When vets graduate, they can't even hope to make the money a doc does. People don't want to be stuck with student loans for the rest of their lives. We're not all Morgans, you know."

"No, but I'd say the Millers have done pretty well for themselves."

"Our parents are scrappers, and education was super important to them. Somehow, they made sure we all went to college where we wanted. They've worked incredibly hard for us."

"You're lucky," he said.

"Yes, we are. That's why my brothers and sisters have pulled together to send them on a trip for their anniversary. They'll kill us, but they've never been anywhere, and we're gonna put 'em on the plane and push it down the runway if we have to."

"Where are they going?"

"Europe, on an extended river cruise. Twenty-six days. Our mom's always wanted to go. They end with four days in Paris."

"If they've never been anywhere, what about passports?" Rich asked, always the practical Morgan son.

Karen grinned, her nose crinkled up. "Last year, I was engaged for a short time. I knew it wasn't going to last, but I held on long enough to begin planning a destination wedding in the West Indies, so they had to get passports. Soon after their passports arrived, the wedding was called off."

"Wow. Remind me not to get engaged to you."

She smiled. "Is that an offer?"

At that moment, they were interrupted by Harriet and Kyle, who were accompanied by Pam's colleague, Elise Nolan. After a moment's conversation, Rich said, "Excuse me, guys. Gotta go catch one of my brothers."

As the handsome eldest Morgan walked away, Karen said," He's a cutie-pie, isn't he?"

"And a *really* nice guy," Harriet said.

Kyle cringed. "Don't tell me my cousin's gonna be your next victim."

Karen gave him a playful punch in the arm. "Not funny."

Harriet smiled at her friend. "Well, you do have a bit of a reputation, dearie."

"People change," Karen said, arm around her.

"Would you excuse me?" Elise asked. "Time to find the ladies'."

"Ultra-deluxe Porta-johns behind the barn," Kyle said.

Elise strolled off, meeting Pam on her way to the Porta-johns. "Hello. What a beautiful night you have," she said.

Pam hugged her colleague. "I can't believe this is the first I'm seeing you."

"I know," Elise said. "I am so sorry to have missed the ceremony. I had an emergency. Slipped in just in time for chowder."

"That's good. No one makes a better chowder than Salters. You having fun?"

Elise nodded. "It's lovely. Simple and fun. The first truly casual wedding I've ever attended."

Pam smiled. "That's my sister and Tim. They knew what they wanted, and they got it."

"They look really happy."

"Yes." Pam noticed her companion's eyes darken. "Is everything okay?"

"There's something I have to tell you. I dated Sandy Rodriguez."

Surprised, Pam recovered herself quickly. "Hasn't every woman in fifty miles?"

"Maybe, but I wanted you to know."

"Because?"

"Because of your relationship with him."

Pam met her friend's dark brown eyes. "There isn't... We have no... Did someone say something to you?"

"No."

"Then how?"

The normally calm, cool Elise's pale cheeks turned red. "I'm sorry. I saw you two earlier and just assumed."

Pam's shoulders relaxed and she breathed out. "Oh, that. That was nothing."

"Didn't look like nothing."

"Well, it was. We did have a brief thing, but it's not going further. Too complicated. I can explain more later."

"No need," Elise said, placing her hand on Pam's arm. "I wanted you to know. Just in case there was something between you. As your colleague and friend, I didn't want you to be blindsided."

"Did you love him?"

The question clearly startled Elise, and she paused, finally saying, "Yes, I did."

"I'm sorry. It seems to be a pattern with him."

"Not necessarily."

Pam regarded her curiously. Even though they shared the office and had become friendly, she didn't know Elise that well. Finally, she said, "Well, thanks for telling me. I appreciate your sensitivity for my feelings."

"Anytime," Elise said. "Now I really must find the ladies' room."

"Just round the corner," Pam said, watching as Elise scurried off. *Small town strikes again!* she mused as she headed to get an ice cream.

Laughing and dancing crazily with her sisters and brothers, Pam had almost forgotten her promise to Sandy. *Almost, but not completely.* Then there was Elise's surprising confession. *What did she see? What did she know?* It was all unsettling.

The Morgan siblings minus Rich and Gail had just finished an embarrassing dance interpretation of "YMCA" when K-Ci and JoJo's moody "All My Life" began. Happy to get off the dance floor and out of sight, Pam was startled when he stepped in front of her, holding out his hand. "You did promise." His smile was warm, with just a hint of mischief.

"Okay, but I warn you after that ridiculous exhibition, I'm drenched in sweat."

"I like sweat," he said, taking her hand and leading her back on the floor.

Oh boy! Pam thought as he drew her into his arms. It felt so good to be held, especially by this man she deeply loved. Loved and couldn't have. *It's only one song*, she thought. *Enjoy every second, then let go.* She rested her head against his chest and sighed.

"That's it, baby. I've got you."

Pam bit back *only for three minutes* as she felt him grow hard against her tummy. Instead of stepping back, she began a rhythmic rubbing against him to the music. It felt so good. She suddenly realized she was panting with lust and desire. No man had ever had this effect on her, and she felt powerless to stop him or herself. When Sandy's hands cruised downward to graze her ass, she gasped.

"Okay there, babe?"

"You did that on purpose!" she whispered, afraid to meet his eyes.

"Oh, and what do you call your bump and grind? You've made me so hard, you're going to have to glue yourself to the front of me till we get off this floor."

"Fat chance of that," she said, her voice saucy as she dared a peek up at him. The coal-black eyes were intense. He wanted her, and it wasn't just lust she saw. It was her own feelings reflected back at her. *Shit, why is life so complicated?*

*****

"So those two are doing a very poor imitation of 'just friends,'" Weezie said to Harriet and Karen, who were watching her sister and Sandy.

"When did that start up?" Harriet said. "They look great together."

"I guess tonight. They had a little thing a month or so ago, but I thought it was kaput."

"Looks pretty intense," Karen said. "Boy, to have that kind of heat and chemistry. Nothing better."

Weezie sighed. "I know… Will I ever find someone like that?"

Others noticed Pam and Sandy, including her father, who whistled. "Oh, to be young again."

Lucy nudged him. "Don't you go all ageist on me, Richard Morgan. Don't forget we're still newlyweds."

"Oh, baby, I'll never forget that or how sexy you are." He drew her close and kissed her temple as Lolly came to stand beside them.

"Hey, partner," Lucy said, circling an arm around her, hoping she hadn't noticed what was happening on the dance floor. *Too late, she had.* Lolly's eyes were riveted on her stepdaughter and her ex-husband. Richard moved away to give the friends some privacy.

"I've been a fool," Lolly said.

Lucy hugged her. "You? Never!"

"Just look at them. In our heyday, he and I never looked like that."

Lucy sighed and held her. There really wasn't anything else to say.

CHAPTER 26

As the music ended, Pam and Sandy held their tight embrace to protect his dignity and because neither one wanted to let go. "That had to be the longest rendition of 'All My Life' I've ever heard," she said, her head still resting on his shoulder.

"I asked them to throw in a couple of extra verses."

She looked up at him, eyes wide. "You didn't."

He grinned as their eyes met. "Had to keep you near me somehow."

Instead of being mad, Pam began to laugh. "And how do you propose we solve our current dilemma? Wanna whistle for a few more verses?" She had stopped her bump and grind, but he was still ready to lose it under those designer jeans of his.

"No, I want to put my hands on those gorgeous hips of yours and follow you straight out of this stuffy old barn."

"Not stuffy, not old. 'Spose I want to make a run for it?"

"You're enjoying this, aren't you?"

Pam smiled. "Kind of."

"So, you going to save me or not?"

"Okay, come on, Casanova." She turned her back to him but stayed close.

As Sandy grabbed her hips, he whispered, "I'm going to get you for that Casanova comment."

"We'll see!" she said merrily. She kept her eyes on the barn floor, afraid to gaze around to see who might be observing.

*****

"Who do they think they're fooling," Raffi said to Coop as they watched his brother and Pam.

"No one," Coop said. "But that was some dance, huh? Why can't I find someone who'll give me a dance like that?"

Across the room, Pam's sisters watched the couple exit the barn. "*Dirty Dancing* has nothing on those two," Weezie said. "If that's what broken up looks like, bring it on!"

"Shush," Gail said. "I'm not sure she picked the most stable person, but we should be happy for her."

"I don't know him," Ava said, "but even from here, that looked like a lot more than lust. Wow, I'll have to go back and think if I ever saw that look in Dan's eyes."

"You're not jealous after your schoolgirl crush on Sandy?" Weezie asked. Only a baby when Sandy had spent the summer in Maine working for her father, she didn't remember Ava following the hunky teenager around, but the story was now part of family lore.

Ava shook her head. "Just the opposite. I have the love of my life, and if he's Pam's, I'm thrilled. But he better not break her heart."

"Or he'll have to answer to all of us," Gail said, finishing her sister's thought.

Nearby, Leonora and Ben Morgan stood with his brother. "You know," Ben said, "we see a fair bit of that out in the valley 'cause someone's always sweet on someone, but boy, they know how to heat up the floor, don't they?"

Richard patted his brother's back, so glad to enjoy this occasion with him. "Who'd a thunk it? That scrawny kid who came to Maine to work for us is out there steaming up my barn with my daughter. Where do you think they're going?"

"You don't want to know, honey," Leonora said.

Her brother-in-law laughed. "I expect you're right, 'cause then I'd have to kill him."

"You okay, dearie?" Harriet asked, finding Elise standing alone. Elise was her therapist, but the women had become friends. Harriet knew of her brief fling with Sandy Rodriguez and she knew how much it had rattled her. They'd been out jogging one afternoon, and Elise had uncharacteristically broken down crying and told Harriet about the relationship.

"Getting there. It's just since then, I've never seen him with another woman, you know?"

"It sucks, doesn't it?"

Elise nodded. "It totally sucks. I mean, I'm happy for them, just ready to go home. It was a great party."

Harriet hugged her and watched as she slipped out a side door into the night.

"Hey, sweetie," Kyle said, putting his arm around her. "Why the long face? Looks like you just lost your best friend."

Harriet smiled at him. "Just concerned for a friend, that's all. I'm fine, especially when your arm's around me."

"Remind me again whose idiotic idea it was to wait so long for this?" He swept out his arm, indicating the party.

"*Both* of ours, 'cause we wanted to do it in Saguaro."

"Well, I can't wait. Want to elope tonight?"

Harriet chuckled, leaning against him. "We're already together. That's all that matters."

"Right as usual, my beautiful fiancée!"

CHAPTER 27

As they rounded the barn, out of sight, Pam stepped ahead out of Sandy's grasp. "There, I think you're safe."

"Not by a long shot," he said, reaching out to her.

Pam put up her arms. "One dance. That was the promise."

"You're honestly going to stand there and tell me that was 'just one dance' after what you were doing to me?"

Pam couldn't see his eyes in the darkness but knew he was right. She'd teased and aroused him on purpose, and for what reason? *Because I want him more than I've ever wanted anyone or anything in my life.* "I might have participated more than I should have, but when you only have one dance, might as well make the best of it."

"Ha-ha. You going to let me kiss you, or do I have to drag you off in the bushes and have my way with you?"

Pam had to admit, she'd loved flirting. Suddenly, she remembered what the consequences could be and took a step back. "Honestly, either of those ideas sounds more than appealing, but neither is a good idea."

He reached out his hand. "Thirty minutes?"

"I can't. Not until Gail and Tim depart. I promised her I'd be there, and I won't let her down."

"How about this? If I promise not to carry you off now, will you promise to meet me here after the bride and groom take off?"

"What would be the point?" she asked, voice quiet.

"That's what we'll find out. I'm settled down now, by the way. Thanks for the escort out."

Every fiber of her being screamed *kiss him, throw yourself in his arms, make wanton, crazy love to him*, but she stepped farther away. "You're welcome. See you later."

"Counting on it," he said.

*****

"There you are!" Gail said as Pam stepped back into the barn. "We're going to dance one more, then take off, okay?"

"I'm here, sis. Gotcha covered," Pam said. "Go dance with hubby."

As the strains of "Sweet Caroline" began, Gail ran off to grab Tim. Pam stood smiling as she watched them, so happy and into each other.

"Well, well, well," Ava said, coming up beside her. "That was quite a show you guys put on."

"What you talking about?" Pam said.

"You two were so lost in each other that I guess you didn't notice everyone watching? Almost upstaged the bride and groom."

Pam's hands shot up to cover her face. "Oh, God, don't tell me that!"

"Relax. I said 'almost,' not 'did.' No one could upstage those two tonight. Gail's on cloud nine, and he's right there with her. However, I'm not sure I'll forgive you for stealing my high school sweetheart."

"You're married, remember? And besides, the year Sandy came to Maine, you were ten, not in high school."

Ava laughed. "Still, it was cool watching you guys. You fit, by the way. He's your yin, sis."

"No, he isn't, and it was one dance."

"Yup, keep telling yourself that."

"Hey, guys," Weezie said, joining them. "I hear it's time to launch the bride and groom. That is if Ms. Sexy Thing has time?"

"Ha-ha," Pam said. "Come on, the dance is ending. Gail needs us."

The four sisters retreated into the house. Gail's overnight bag was by the front door, and she wasn't changing, so there really wasn't much to do except hug each other and congratulate the bride one more time.

Gail looked from one to the other of her sisters and said, "Thanks. I couldn't have done it without you three. I still have to pinch myself to see if all this is real. Remember what a bitch I was when Dad first proposed selling the farm and moving down here?"

"Yup," Weezie said.

"Well, I sure was wrong. If Ava hadn't paved the way and introduced Dad to this place, I'd have never met Tim."

Pam took her hands. "Well, you have, and you're a married woman now, so let's get you on your way. Your gorgeous, amazing husband is waiting."

Armed with cups of birdseed, the guests heralded Gail and Tim's departure. As they reached his truck, Richard stepped forward and gave Gail a hug. "So happy for you, princess," he whispered.

"Thanks, Dad," she said, tears in her eyes.

Faith and Rex Miller hugged the couple, and then they were off into the night for the short drive to the Oceanside.

Pam stood with her sisters and brothers, uncertain of where Sandy was in the crowd. She hadn't spotted him when they walked Gail out, and now he seemed to have disappeared. "What do you think?" Ava said. "Have we got room for one more ice cream?"

"Not me," Pam said. "I'm stuffed." *And I have a promise to keep.* As her sisters headed for the dessert table, she wandered around to the back of the barn, where the gleaming luxury Porta-johns sat.

"Not the most romantic spot," he said from behind her. "Let's go this way." Before she could speak, Sandy took her hand and began down the path that led to the corrals and stables.

"And you think a barn full of manure is better?"

"Ah, but I've done my homework, babe," he said. "There's a loft in your dad's fancy horse barn, and it's filled with clean, sweet hay."

"I've never seen it," Pam said.

"Well, this is a first, then. Come on."

He pulled her into the barn to the ladder to the loft. Hand on the ladder, she turned to him. "I'm not sure about this. I mean we don't… I've never—"

His lips captured hers, tongue thrusting deep as he drew her close, knocking the air out of her. Pam opened herself to him, returning the kiss, her tongue teasing, the taste of him intoxicating. When he finally released her, lips on her slender neck, he said, "Did that convince you, or do you need more?"

Pam nodded and turned to climb the ladder, his magnetic, hot presence urging her forward. When they reached the top, moonlight streamed through the far window, illuminating the hay-filled space. Before she could speak, his mouth captured hers and he scooped her up in his arms, carrying her forward, laying her on the soft hay.

"This is our night, baby," he said, voice husky as his hands reached under her shirt, teasing one breast, then the other until she moaned with her first release. *This is going to be an amazing thirty minutes!*

Pam unbuttoned her shirt and slipped it and her bra off, laying them underneath her against the hay that prickled her soft skin. "That's my girl," he said, mouth taking one, then the other breast, licking and sucking until she was moaning again.

With lightning speed, he removed her jeans and panties, then his own. He lay his shirt under them as his fingers moved between her legs. "Tell me what you want sweetie"

"You inside me now," she managed, delirious with desire as her body rammed against him, begging.

"Patience, my little sexpot." His fingers found her clit, driving her almost blind with a second orgasm. "You're a slick, hot little thing, aren't you? Sure you're ready for me?"

In answer, Pam grabbed his ass and drew him down until his cock bumped against her. "Whoa, baby, one sec." He slipped a condom on and kissed her deeply as he perched above her. "What do you think? Want to try something?"

"As long as it involves you inside of me immediately!" she said, shocked at her boldness.

With one easy movement, he flipped her, and Pam found herself kneeling in the soft hay. "Oh, boy," she said as he entered her, slowly, languidly, gently.

"Is this okay?" he asked.

"No, harder, deeper," she gasped. "Want more, much more."

As Sandy obliged, ramming into her, Pam pushed back against him, urging him deeper and deeper until he wondered if he'd ever come back. "Oh, babe, oh my sweet babe," he said, making love like he never had before.

As the moonlight streamed in, lighting their bodies, they moved in delicious synchrony to a heart-stopping crescendo. She released first, and as soon as Sandy felt her orgasm, he let go as well. As their passion cooled, he wrapped his arms around her and gently moved them onto their sides, maintaining their sweet connection. "Oh, geez, baby, that was incredible. Thank you." He kissed the back of her neck softly and felt her embrace his cock deep inside her.

"That's my most erogenous zone," she whispered.

"Good to know," he said, kissing her again and again.

As Pam felt his cock harden, she murmured, "Mmm," and pushed back against him, urging him on.

"You're on," he whispered as he slipped on a fresh condom and their dance began again, this time longer, more gently, until they hit a peak and sweet, explosive release.

Afterward, they rested a few minutes, until she said, "Much as I'd kill to stay here all night, I've got to get back."

In answer, he trailed soft kisses up and down her neck.

"No, no!" she said, moaning as she moved away from him.

"Geez, you're cruel," he said, rolling around and sitting up. "Now to find our goddamn clothes. They must be everywhere."

With horses nickering softly below them, they searched by the light of his cell phone, finally locating everything except her panties. "Forget them," she said finally, pulling on her jeans. "I'll come get them in the morning."

They scurried down and exited the barn. Guests were still standing around, mostly family. He drew her into his arms for a brief kiss. "I'd prolong the kiss, but then I'd have to drag you back to the hayloft," he said, grinning down at her.

Pam placed her hands on his chest, loving his warmth and the feel of his heart beating. "And we can't have that, can we?"

"That was the most amazing experience of my life."

"Mine too."

"So where do we go from here?"

As Pam stepped away, she wondered, *Where indeed. After that, there's no way I can say goodbye.* "Let's see."

"About?"

"About I don't know," she said.

"Okay, this is what I propose. You've got wedding stuff and family around tomorrow. Let's get together Monday night. The club's closed. I'll think of something and give you a call. Sound okay?"

She nodded, not trusting her voice at that moment.

"Night, baby."

"Night," Pam said, turning away and hurrying toward the open barn door.

CHAPTER 28

Tim's aunts Grace and Hope Childs hosted a brunch Sunday in Grace's backyard. Hope had never married, and Grace was widowed with one daughter, Cora, who lived in Scotland. A travel writer, Cora never stayed in one place very long. She loved her cousin Tim and had come for the wedding before going on an assignment to Newfoundland. "Hi, welcome," she said as the Morgans arrived in three cars along with Spark and Helen. "For those I didn't meet yesterday, I'm Cora. My mom and Aunt Grace are over there somewhere." She pointed to a small tent under which a few tables had been haphazardly arranged.

"Typical aunts. We'll be lucky if they remembered to get food." Pam was startled by a voice at her shoulder and turned to find Rex Miller, Junior, Tim's brother, followed by Karen and Brick.

Pam nodded to them. "Good morning. How's the Miller family today?"

"Partied out," Rex said.

"Ignore him, ladies," Karen said to Pam and Weezie. "He's the party pooper of the family. Did anyone see him dancing last night? I don't think so!" Karen leaned forward, whispering, "Speaking of dancing, that was quite a dance you had with Sandy Rodriguez."

Pam's face blazed. "Would you excuse me for just a sec?"

As her sister hurried off toward where Tim and Gail stood talking to his parents, Weezie said, "Touchy subject."

Karen laughed. "I guess so."

Pam stood beside the newlyweds, her thoughts swirling. *What was I thinking? Am I completely insane? I've become involved with one of the town's biggest playboys. Not only will I be the talk of the whole village, but Lolly LaSalle's probably sharpening her claws as she prepares to take him to court!*

"Hey, mornin', darlin'," Spark Foster said, giving her a bear hug. "Don't you look pretty."

She gave him a wan smile. "Thanks, Spark."

"Why the long face, sweetie?"

"It's a long story complete with embarrassment, gossip, and insanity."

He grinned, winking as Helen stepped away to see if she could help the hosts, who were her dear friends and fellow Darn Yarners. "Wouldn't have anything to do with your red-hot dance last night, would it?"

"So you saw it too? I was hoping there might be one soul at the wedding who had been otherwise occupied and hadn't observed it."

He chuckled. "Wouldn't have missed it for the world, darlin'. Best thing I've seen since our last Valley dance. Someone's always smokin' up the floor at those. I loved it. Reminded me of my dancin' days with my wife, Patsy. Boy, did we love to dance, and we could really generate heat, I can tell you. Just ask your Uncle Ben. In fact, he and Nora were always smokin' hot too. Still are."

"You're just trying to make me feel better."

"Not a bit of it. When people are in love, there's no quenching those flames. And who'd want to?"

Helen returned. After a few minutes' conversation, Pam excused herself to join her family. Food did eventually appear, and most guests filled their paper plates and came to sit on the lawn. People dropped in and out, and Pam spied several of Sandy's siblings, but he did not appear. It was his day with Maisie.

Ava and Dan's kids were cranky and tired, so they packed up shortly after lunch. Pam had come with them and was happy to escape. After they dropped her off, she decided to take a run.

*****

As Spark and Helen drove back to her cottage, he said, "It's been a great weekend, darlin'. When we gonna see you in Saguaro?"

"Probably not until the wedding."

"I can send the plane anytime, you know."

"Dear Spark, you really know how to turn a gal's head."

"I hope so. And you're a special gal."

Silence ensued. The silence of acceptance for where they were and what they had together—a dear friendship that could probably never be more. Too many ghosts, too many shadows, and they had both given their whole heart to another. For life, even after death.

As they turned up the drive to Helen's cottage, she said, "Thank you."

"Back atcha, darlin'. Always."

*****

The day was warm with a lovely breeze as Pam headed down Beach Road toward the end of the peninsula. She hadn't run for over a week, and it felt wonderful. When she reached the edge of Land's End and the Miller property, she decided to keep going a ways on the eighteen-mile bridle path that ringed the peninsula. She hadn't gone far when she spied horses ahead. As the riders neared her, she saw it was Karen Miller and Harriet Winthrop.

"Hey, ladies," she said as they reached her. "Great afternoon for a ride."

"Hi Pam," Harriet said. "Are you enjoying a little downtime after the busy weekend?"

Pam smiled. "Something like that. There's a family dinner tonight, so I'm grabbing a few hours while I can. Are you coming to that?"

"We'll probably stop by, but Kyle's working."

"Oh?"

Karen nodded. "We've got two foals coming at Land's End, and it's looking like tonight's the night."

"Oh my goodness, how exciting," Pam said. "A vet's work is never done, I guess."

"He loves every minute of it," Harriet said.

"And we love him," Karen said. "Hey, we just passed your boyfriend and Maisie."

"Excuse me?"

Harriet noticed Pam's face drop and quickly said, "They're riding bikes along the trail."

Pam gazed behind them. There was no one in sight. "Well, probably time for me to turn around. I'll let you two go first."

"Have a good run!" Karen called as Harriet smiled and waved goodbye.

As soon as the women were out of sight, Pam turned and picked up her pace, headed toward home. She couldn't exactly say why, but she did not want to encounter father and daughter just now. As she reached the end of the trail and hit Beach Road, she let out a sigh. *Almost there*, she thought, slowing down.

About a hundred yards from her house, she heard laughter behind her and turned to see Sandy and Maisie. "Hey!" he called as they approached.

Pam stopped to wait for them. "Hi," she said as they stopped alongside her.

Maisie smiled, looking from her to her father. She was a beautiful child with dark curly hair and dimples. Tiny glasses framed her chocolate-brown eyes. "I'm Maisie!"

Pam smiled warmly. "I'm Pam. So nice to meet you."

"Are you a friend of my daddy's?"

"Yes, I am," she said with a quick glance at him.

"Do you live here?"

"Right there." Pam pointed behind her at the house.

"Can we come in?"

"Maisie, whoa—Pam is probably busy."

"As a matter of fact, I do have to take a shower and be somewhere in an hour, but if you guys need a quick glass of water, you're welcome to come in."

"Please, Daddy?"

Sandy met her eyes, and her libido did a flip-flop. *Wow, does he ever fill out a pair of biking shorts!*

"Are you sure?" he asked.

"Absolutely. Come in, please."

They set their bikes inside her fence and followed her up to the porch. As soon as she opened the door, Maisie ran past her. "Not at all shy," he said. "Sorry."

"She's delightful," Pam said, conscious of his warmth and musky scent beside her. "Thanks."

They followed the child through the house, where she had found the back porch. "This is like Daddy's! I wish we lived on the river."

"Who'd like water, or lemonade?" Pam asked.

They chose lemonade, and she brought three glasses out to the porch, where Maisie was perched at the railing, scanning the river bottom for crabs. She gazed up at Pam with big brown eyes sparkling. "Hey, do you have a net?"

"I think there might be one in the shed," Pam said.

Sandy raised his hand. "Not today, peanut. Pam's busy, so we're only stayin' a minute. We can do crab patrol at my house."

"I don't mind looking for the net," she said. "I love crabbing."

"Please, Daddy?"

Sandy grinned. "Ten minutes, and I'll look for the net. You ladies stay here."

Pam and Maisie sipped their lemonade and chatted, gazing over the railing and pointing as one or the other spotted movement in the eel grass below. A few minutes later, he returned with a long-poled net and handed it to Maisie. "Now hold on tight, peanut. We don't want to lose Pam's net."

Pam smiled. "Technically it's the Fergusons' net, but somehow I don't think they'd mind. They'd be pleased that someone's using it."

As Maisie trolled the bottom trying to scoop up crabs, her father stood behind her, ready to catch the net handle. Suddenly, the child shrieked, "Got one!" and brought up the net.

A small green crab flailed in the webbing until Sandy turned the handle and dumped it on the deck. As Maisie jumped up and down, the crab skittered across the wood slats. "Stop him, Daddy! Stop him!"

Sandy reached down and picked up the crab, holding it by the stomach, out of reach of its claws. Gently, he handed it to Maisie, who held it at arm's length, studying it. He looked at Pam, a proud father look that melted her heart. *How could I ever come between this?*

Pam shook off the wave of sadness and said, "You are an expert crab catcher *and* handler, aren't you?"

"Daddy taught me."

"He also taught you 'catch and release.' Time to let him go, baby."

The child looked at Pam. "Think it'll hurt him to fall so far? We usually take 'em down the steps at Daddy's."

Pam picked up the net. "Why don't we put him back in the net, and you can lower him down slowly?"

As the three of them watched the crab drift downward and disappear into the eel grass, Sandy said, "Time to go, peanut. Pam's busy. Drink up your lemonade."

She walked them to their bikes, brushing against him as they followed Maisie. Just a slight touch, and his warmth ignited sensations everywhere. Pam grabbed the porch railing to steady herself, at the same time wishing they would touch again. *How will I ever stay warm without him?*

After adjusting Maisie's helmet and donning his own, Sandy straddled his bike. "Thanks. We needed that lemonade to get us the last half mile, didn't we, peanut?"

"My pleasure," Pam said, waving as they headed off, giving her an excellent view of his great ass and strong, muscular back. *Yikes!*

CHAPTER 29

"Love it, love it, love it when we're all together," Richard said. With Lucy by his side, they had all eight of his children, her two, Tim Miller and the Saguaro contingent, and Lucy's mom. Sunday dinner was roast lamb with spring vegetables and a huge field greens salad. Callie had gotten all sorts of breads and rolls from the Café, and baskets of these lined the table along with dishes of herb-infused olive oils and sweet butter.

"I hear you, brother," Ben Morgan said, reaching over to squeeze his wife's hand. "My Nora and I are never happier than when all of ours are under one roof."

"Although that's getting a little trickier as the family grows," Leonora said. "Between grandchildren and all our new kids marrying into the family, we'd have to build another house to accommodate everyone."

"We consider the ranch our home, including the cabins and kids' properties, so between us all, there are plenty of beds," her husband said.

Spark chuckled. "Don't you New England folks worry a bit. I've got so many bedrooms at my house, I've lost count."

Helen smiled. "He sure does."

Richard's son Ben said, "Hey, Uncle, we may have to create some nicknames for December. How many Bens will there be?"

"Well, there's you, son, then our three including me. We call the little one Bennie, so it's just you, your cousin, and me who'll be confusin'."

Leonora patted her husband's arm. "Honestly, honey, it's the tone of voice that gives the biggest clue. I'm just getting to know you, but I have definite inflections in my voice when talking to my husband or son."

"Hmm…I look forward to hearing all that in action and how you'll distinguish me," Ben said.

"Very cordially," Ben Senior said.

"So enough about us old folks," Leonora said. "How are the newlyweds? Are you all packed and ready to go?"

Gail beamed. "We are. We're so excited." She leaned against Tim's shoulder.

"A week in paradise," Richard said. "Nothing more spectacular than Arcadia at this time of year."

Gail and Tim linked hands, smiling at one another. Pam watched them, so happy for her sister, yet heartbroken that she had walked away from love.

"Yes, and as I told Tim. I'm thrilled that I never have to date again!" Gail said, her face clouding as she spied her sister. She tried to make eye contact, but Pam looked away.

Leonora spotted the interaction and said, "Dating does have its perks and is full of so many possibilities! Just look at all these lucky singles around this beautiful table."

Talk turned to catching up on the schedule for Teddy's latest exhibition, which several of them planned to attend. Pam's brother did large-scale metal-and-stone sculptures. His work was beginning to create a buzz outside of Providence, but the upcoming exhibition was to be in Roger Williams Park, and two of the twelve featured works were to be part of the park's permanent installations.

As Callie laid out desserts on the buffet, Gail and Tim rose. "Sorry, everyone," she said, arm circling his waist. "We promised the Miller clan we'd join them for dessert."

They hugged everyone, saying their goodbyes. They were staying at Tim's apartment for the night and leaving at dawn for Maine. Gail found Pam and whispered, "I'm sorry, sweetie."

"For what?"

"For my really thoughtless blurting about dating."

"It wasn't thoughtless at all. You're happy, and I'm happy for you. Thrilled, in fact. And as a member of the lucky dating crowd, I'm looking forward to all my perks," she whispered, well out of earshot of their aunt.

"She's something, isn't she?" Gail said. "Have a great dinner tomorrow. Where's he taking you?"

"He won't tell me. He and his daughter stopped by this afternoon for some crabbing."

"Oh?"

"Oh nothing. She's a cutie, his Maisie."

"I'll be thinking of you!" Gail said, giving her one more hug.

"You better not be. This is your honeymoon!"

"Bye, sis," she said, kissing her and flying off to join Tim.

As people dispersed, Lucy said goodbye to her mother and Spark, assuring them that Amy would be packed and ready bright and early when the driver arrived for their airport trip. She then found Pam in the kitchen helping Callie put dishes away. "How you doing?" she asked.

"Great, fine. Happy for Gail and Tim."

"I meant how are *you* doing?" Lucy said.

"I know what you mean, but it's easiest to avoid the subject right now."

"It won't always be like this. Lolly'll settle down. In fact, all she needs is a little romance of her own, and she'll forget all about you and Sandy."

"So you're saying I should be patient till a man sweeps her off her feet? Or maybe I should get busy and round up some suitable dates for her?"

Lucy smiled. "Not at all. I just mean that my dear friend isn't very happy right now, so she'll take it out on whoever's a convenient target."

"Well, I don't relish being a target. Probably better for me to get out of the line of fire."

"Even if he's the one?"

"Even then. And let's face it, I don't know if he's the one. He has a terrible reputation as a Lothario, not to mention a cheating spouse. Do people like him ever change?"

Lucy sighed. "You're asking the wrong person. As someone with a cheating ex, I can tell you it's pretty dreadful. Hard to get past, especially when you thought the marriage was happy."

"But was his and Lolly's?"

"Truthfully? Never…or maybe for a few months. She had a long-time boyfriend who treated her very badly. When they broke up, Sandy came along, and Lolly jumped into the deep end. She was beautiful. Still is. I don't think Sandy knew what hit him. By the time he did, they were married and living back here. Miserably, I might add. They're very different. Only thing that they really had in common was Maisie, but Lolly suffered horrendous postpartum depression for over a year after Maisie's birth. That further estranged them.

"Sandy tried so hard, but she wouldn't let him near her. Cut him off, blamed him for her wild mood swings. I love Lolly. She's a dear, dear friend, but we were all at the end of our ropes with her. She wouldn't see a therapist, refused all meds, and pretty much stayed holed up in her bedroom."

"What about work?"

"I hired people to help me. She couldn't do it."

"Sounds very sad."

"It was, because she's an amazing person. Believe me, I don't condone cheating after what I went through, but I can't say I completely blame Sandy for seeking companionship elsewhere. He put up with a lot of shit before he strayed."

"Still not right."

Lucy squeezed her shoulder. "No I 'spose not. I'd better go see what your father's up to. Want to come?"

"Thanks, but I think I'll take a walk."

Ava, Dan and the kids had gone home, but Pam found her brothers and Weezie sitting in the family room. "How'd you get over here, Wolfie?" she asked.

"Walked, and I'm about to head back."

"Good, then come on, guys and gals. Let's walk to the winery. I'd love the exercise after that meal and don't want to brave the coyotes alone on the return trip."

As they followed the mile-long gravel road to the winery, the siblings chatted, laughed and admired the stars. Rich, Pam, and Weezie didn't get much time with Teddy and Ben, so it was fun to catch up away from their father's hovering. They all adored Richard Morgan, but he had taken his role as sole parent very seriously over the years. Sometimes his oversight could be stifling. If asked, none of them would have had it any other way, but they felt like "just kids" alone together, especially the older ones, who remembered life before their mother's death.

CHAPTER 30

Monday, Pam popped into the office to meet with Elise between her colleague's clients. "Morning!" she called, the inner office door open as she stepped in.

"In here! Tea water's hot!' Elise called.

Pam shut the door behind her, hung up her jacket, and headed into the warm, inviting consulting room. As they sank into the overstuffed armchairs, hot mugs of Earl Grey in hand, she sighed. "I will miss this cozy space."

Elise set down her mug. "We can make the new spaces just as cozy." They were moving to the bottom floor of a recently restored building at the east end of the village, just across the street from Laura's Community Garden. Once a home, the office building was now zoned commercial and the interior spaces repurposed. They would be sharing the building with two acupuncturists. whose rooms were on the second floor. and an accountant, Andy Roby, whose office was at the back of the first floor. The building had a kitchen and bathroom on the first floor, and the huge front parlor had been divided into two consulting rooms for Pam and Elise. The smaller parlor just inside the front door served as the waiting room for them and the other tenants. They had debated about whether this was appropriate given the differing natures of the businesses, but after taking a survey of their current patients, they found that no one objected to the arrangement.

"Yes, we can. If you'd like to come, I'm thinking of hitting furniture and antique stores in Bayport later this week to find chairs, tables, and a few rugs for my consulting space. I was also thinking we should contribute a sofa and maybe a chair or two to the waiting room?"

"I'm booked solid," Elise said, "but I trust you and am happy to contribute to the common spaces. Andy says he's bringing a coffeemaker, a fridge, and a bunch of shelves."

Pam watched her colleague set her tea down with shaky hands. Elise looked ashen, and her clothes seemed to hang on her already thin frame. "You okay? You look pale."

Elise waved her hand dismissively. "Seasonal allergies, no biggie."

"Should we talk about the wedding?"

"Not unless you want to," Elise said, dark eyes meeting Pam's.

"I just don't want… I mean, with us growing this business and all… I don't want things to be weird between us."

"I promise they won't. Sometimes it just hits me, you know?"

"I do know, but the relationship between Sandy and me is not going anywhere. I'm going to tell him as much tonight."

"Then you're crazy. Why would you do that?"

"Because I won't come between him and his child, and I hate, hate, hate strife. I'd rather walk away now and avoid the mess."

Elise put up her hands in mock protest. "Okay, okay, I'm not gonna lie. I was, and maybe still am, in love with Sandy Rodriguez, but he *never* looked at me the way he looks at you. Anyone can see he's crazy in love with you. And, as you should well know, relationships are *always* messy. *Always.* Even the best ones."

"Well then, I'll never have one, 'cause I can't stand messy!"

They talked and planned until Elise's client arrived, then Pam headed out. She wanted to stop by the new building and then the garden. It was close to noon, so she ducked into the Café and grabbed a drink and one of the prepared sandwiches, an egg salad on rye. When she stepped into the building, she heard movement at the back of the building and then Andy Roby, the accountant, emerged.

"Hey, Pam, how're you doin'?" Andy was short and a little pudgy with sandy-blond hair and green eyes, dressed in rumpled khakis and a gray T-shirt. His face and hands were smudged with dirt.

"Great. You moving in?"

"Sort of. They did a great job of cleaning everything except the closets. They weren't cleaned, vacuumed, dusted, nothin'. I've been workin' in mine. I think I'm gonna hire Kev Averill to paint it."

"Let me take a look at ours," she said, disappearing into her consulting room. Sure enough, the closet she shared with Elise was filthy and untouched.

Andy was still waiting with rags in hand when she emerged. "Yes, please ask Kev to do ours too. I don't care what color, just so it's clean."

"Will do. I'm headin' over there now, then to get lunch. Can I grab you something?"

She held up her Café bag. "Got it. I'm actually headed for the garden. Just wanted to take a few quick measurements."

"How was the wedding?"

"Great. Busy, fun. Gail and Tim are off on their honeymoon."

"Karen's crazy about your sister, or her sister, as she calls her."

"That's right, Tim's sister works for you."

He nodded. "Couple of days a week when I can get her. Glad the wedding was fun. Always nice when two great people find each other," he said. "You seeing anyone?" Andy was recently divorced, and his eyes reflected a sad longing.

Pam hesitated. She would ordinarily have said "no," but didn't want to encourage an overture from Andy. "Yes, I am."

"Too bad, or I'd ask you out. Is that other pretty sister of yours dating?"

Pam laughed. "Weezie? Always."

"Just my luck. Well, I'd better get crackin'. Gotta be back at the old office to see clients in an hour. This week was supposed to be my vacation."

Pam walked across the street to the garden, now half-planted. The beautiful sign "Laura's Community Garden" now hung at the entrance. She sighed with pleasure as she passed through the arbor, the scent of sweet geraniums all around her. A few gardeners were working as she strolled through, stopping to say hello. At the far end, she found a bench in the shade and sat. Two of their most reliable volunteers were watering, and another raked the paths.

Watching all the activity, she sighed again. *How many people get to see their dream become reality?*

CHAPTER 31

He had said "casual," so Pam showered and dressed in clean skinny jeans, a soft peach-colored top, silver earrings and bracelet, and a pair of striped espadrilles. She brushed her hair, allowing it to fall loose over her shoulders and applied a hint of lipstick. "Very nice," she said to herself as she passed the hall mirror. She went through the house and decided to wait on the deck. It was a calm night, and the river flowed by. relaxing her somewhat frayed nerves. *Say what you have to say, be firm, and walk away*, she mused, closing her eyes.

The doorbell's ring startled her, and she realized she'd fallen asleep for a few minutes. Shaking herself, she padded through the house in bare feet, her espadrilles waiting near the front door.

"Wow!" Sandy said as he spied her. "You look sensational, as always."

She bit back her automatic *I do not*, and said, "Thanks, you look pretty sensational yourself." And he did in shorts and an open-collared sport shirt almost the same color as her top.

He grabbed hold of his shirtsleeve. "Hey, we could be the Bobbsey Twins."

She arched an eyebrow, meeting his eyes. "You know about the Bobbsey Twins?"

"I had sisters and friends who were obsessed with 'em."

"I think they're more from our parents' generation."

"You forget, I'm a tad older than you. A tween, maybe?"

She laughed, slipping into her shoes. "Am I okay for where we're going?"

"You're perfect."

He had the Audi, which she slid into, the wonderful scent of leather mixing with his scent—spices and musk. "Is it a far drive?"

He grinned, kissing her cheek. "Not at all."

Pam had just settled into the soft seat and was admiring his muscular legs when he turned a corner and swung into his driveway. "Here we are!"

"Your house?"

"Yup."

"But… I thought we—"

"I can cook, don't worry."

"It's not that. It's just—"

"And I won't jump you the second we walk in. Come on. Let's just have a nice relaxing time together, okay?"

He reached out his hand to help her from the car. The warmth of his touch instantly raised her body temperature to boiling. *Deep breaths, Pam Morgan. Take deep calming breaths.*

"Did you say something, babe?"

"No, nothing." *Great, now he's a mind reader!*

As he led her through the house, she spied the table set intimately, two places catty corner. Delicious smells wafted from the kitchen. "Something smells incredible," she said.

"I hope so. It's my specialty—cioppino, an Italian bouillabaisse. It's all set. Just have to add the seafood at the last minute. What can I get you to drink? I have pretty much everything."

"What wine would you suggest with the cioppino, which I adore, by the way?"

"I have a really good Chianti. We could also begin with gin and tonics? It's kind of a gin and tonic night, don't you think?"

Pam smiled. "If you say so. Please make mine weak, with lots of lime."

"Coming right up!"

They settled on the deck, sitting side by side on the longer porch glider. "I love this," she said, patting the seat. "It reminds me of one we had in Maine."

"My grandmother had one on her porch when we were kids. It got lost or broken over the years, but I had this made from how I remembered it."

"It's heaven," she said, leaning back, her head resting on the cushion.

Sandy reached over and gently rubbed her thigh. "Thanks for coming."

She gazed over at him and saw her own desire and lust reflected in his dark eyes. She took a deep breath. "I haven't changed my mind."

"Okay. But we can be friends, right?"

"Yes."

They chatted about their day as the glider swung gently. Sandy excused himself a couple of times to check on dinner. Each time he returned, he managed to inch a little closer to her until their arms touched as they swung.

"This is nice," she said, warmed by the gin and his presence beside her.

"Sure is," he said, reaching over and taking her hand.

His fingers gently massaged her palm sending shivers of sensation through her. "Your Maisie is adorable, by the way," she said, endeavoring to repress her rising desire to leap into his arms and scream, *Take me!*

"She's a good kid."

"Sandy… I…I want to…say—"

"Hold that thought," he said as his iWatch pinged. "Dinner's ready." He jumped up, letting go of her hand.

Pam felt as if she'd been set adrift in a cold, lonely ocean. She followed him into the kitchen.

"You sit, please," he said, setting an open bottle of Chianti on the table.

As she watched, he tossed a salad, set crusty bread in a basket, then ladled the cioppino into two large, colorful pottery soup bowls. "Here you go," he said, setting hers in front of her. He set out the salad and bread, with olive oil and butter for the bread.

As he watched, Pam raised a spoonful to her lips. "Oh my goodness, this is amazing!"

He grinned. "Glad you like it."

"It's the best cioppino, bouillabaisse, or any kind of fish stew I've ever had."

They ate in silence for a few minutes, enjoying the delicious food. She took a sip of wine and sighed. "A talented cook among your many other qualities."

"It was either learn to cook or starve. I don't do junk food, and takeout has to be really good and really healthy for me to indulge."

"Don't you offer food at the club?"

"Honestly, mostly crap, although we do get sandwiches and salads from the Café. The appetizers are junk, but that's what people want."

"You must be really proud of Sandy's. It's one of the premier music venues on the East Coast."

"Yeah, it's a cool place. Was fun to build it, and I have good people working for me. I'm actually getting restless and thinking about something new. Murph runs the place, and the only reason I'm there half the time is that the bigger groups insist on being welcomed and introduced by me."

Pam smiled. "Your name is why they come, right?"

"They come because we get great crowds of people who know and love music."

She nodded. "This really is incredible," she said, setting her spoon beside her bowl.

Sandy rose, cleared their plates, and then served small flans with a chocolate drizzle and fresh raspberries. Pam took a bite and sighed. "Mmm… One of my favorites."

"Mine too," he said. "So we've talked about your garden—which is amazing, by the way—and my business and our day-to-day activities. What about us?"

He reached over and took her hand. Pam's body responded immediately to his loving touch, the heat coursing through her. She sat up, squeezed his hand, then withdrew hers from his grasp. "There isn't any us. There can't be."

"Excuse my language, but that's bullshit."

Surprised by his tone, she looked up to find his eyes blazing. He was angry and something else. Hurt? Desperate? "Maybe it's time for me to go."

"Pam, please. I'm dying here. At least have a drink before you go. Anything—coffee, tea, water, brandy, whatever."

She stayed seated, swallowing another bite of flan. It was a shame to waste it, but she no longer tasted or appreciated it. Her mind and body were in turmoil, and all she wanted to do was run. "Okay, a tea would be great."

"Good. I'll heat water."

He put on the kettle, then returned as they ate dessert in silence. Afterward, he led her out to the deck, setting the tea on the table in front of the glider. They sipped their teas for a few minutes until he broke the silence. "Talk to me."

"I have very strong feelings for you. I do. I also have a healthy set of fears based on your reputation and past behavior. But all that is beside the point. I will not come between you and Maisie."

"But—"

Pam put up her hand. "I can't explain it, but I don't like strife. I run from it. Like quitting my school job… I couldn't do it with that fear hanging over every day. Then there are relationships, which are always messy and scary."

He set down his mug. "They don't have to be."

"But this one is."

"Listen, Pam, I have equally strong feelings for you. I love you. It's different from the way I've ever felt about any other woman, including Lolly in our early days. This is not sweet talk, I promise. As extraordinary as it is, it's not the sex. It's you. I do not want you to walk out of my life."

"That's hardly going to happen when we live in the same town."

"You know what I mean," he said, reaching out to take her hand.

"Yes, I do, but this is all I can do right now. I'm so sorry," Pam said, withdrawing her hand, her body on fire with longing. There was a tingling in the pit of her stomach, and she wondered how she could escape gracefully when all she wanted to do was throw herself into his arms.

"Pam, please."

Abruptly, she stood. "I can't… I have to go." She took her mug into the kitchen, placing it hastily in the sink, then grabbing her bag.

"This is ridiculous," he said, grasping her arm. "Please stay."

Pam shook her head, afraid to speak lest she burst into tears. Her misery settled like a steel weight on her chest. "I can't." She pulled away from his grasp and ran to the front hall, throwing open the door.

As she stood outside, tears clouding her vision, she remembered that he had driven her here. *No matter, the walk will do me good.* She turned toward home and began walking. Sandy followed her, jumping into his car and cruising up alongside her.

"At least let me take you home."

"No, thanks. The walk feels good."

"Pam wait!."

She continue walking, afraid to look in his direction. "Go home, Sandy. Please."

He continued alongside her for a half mile, then turned around. "Night," he called as he headed the Audi toward home.

Ice spread through Pam's stomach as he disappeared. *What have I done?*

CHAPTER 32

The next few weeks were filled with meetings, new client appointments, and garden chores. Pam pushed through each day, telling herself that things would get better soon, but they didn't. Despite full days with friends, family, and fellow gardeners, she felt bereft and lonely. Twice a day, morning and evening, Sandy called, but she let her phone go to voicemail. She would listen to his messages, tears streaming as the strong, familiar voice told her he loved her and missed her.

Given Elise's history with Sandy, she avoided talking to her, but finally made an appointment with a therapist in Bayport whom Frankie recommended.

"Welcome, Ms. Morgan," Carroll Ranglund said, ushering her into her consulting room. The short middle-aged therapist was dressed in sensible khakis, a moss-green twin sweater set, and loafers. Her salt-and-pepper hair was styled in a tight pageboy.

"It's Pam, please. Thank you for seeing me on such short notice."

"My pleasure. Frankie's a dear friend. How can I help?"

Pam poured out the story of Sandy and her relationship as well as her weeks of anguish and sadness. She ended by saying, "I don't know how to get beyond this, Ms. Ranglund."

"It's Carroll. What outcome are you seeking?"

"Peace, I guess. Yes, to be peaceful and to have my life back the way it was before I met him. To stop thinking about him day and night."

"Why do you think you can't let go?"

"I love him."

"Knowing that, what steps might you take to get your life back?"

Pam shrugged. "Well, I could travel. That's what my sister Gail did when her relationship went south."

"Did it work?"

"She's married to the guy now."

"So did the travel help her sort things out?"

"I don't know. They had very different issues, and Tim's a very different person from Sandy."

"Is that significant?"

Pam shrugged. "Depends on how you look at it. Tim had a reputation as a bit of a Lothario too."

"Is that why you're staying away from Sandy?"

"Yes… No… I don't know. That's why I'm here."

"So is it really the issues around his daughter that keep you away?"

"No, it's the messiness. I don't like conflict. I'd rather hide in a hole than deal with conflict and anger."

"Where is this conflict and anger?" Carroll said.

"Well, there's his ex-wife's raging, and also Sandy's. He's furious that I won't try to work through things."

"Is that bad?"

Pam shook her head. "Hell if I know. I just know I don't like anyone's anger directed at me."

"Why do you think he's angry?"

"Because he's not getting what he wants."

"Is that what you truly think?"

Pam gazed over at her. "No," she said in quiet voice.

"So why is he angry?"

"Because he's frustrated. And because he thinks he loves me."

"Thinks?"

"How can a man like that know what love is?"

"Happens all the time."

"What?"

Carroll smiled. "Men and women go from relationship to relationship, and then suddenly, they find the one."

"How would I know if this is the case here?"

"You don't. Falling in love and committing to an intimate relationship does involve an element of risk."

"Not one of my favorite things, risk."

"Can you think of any time in your life when you have been willing to take a risk?"

"Well, there was learning to ride a bike, then a horse. I was terrified. Then there's collaborating in a therapy practice and taking the big step with the new building. And, of course, the garden. So many pieces had to fit together to create it."

"You haven't discussed your biking and horseback riding, but it sounds like the other things have been very successful and have brought you a sense of accomplishment and maybe joy?"

"But I didn't risk my heart."

Carroll smiled. "Hearts are muscles, and they are really quite resilient. More resilient and much stronger than we can imagine."

"Then why has mine ached so much the past few weeks?"

"Perhaps because you're fighting so hard against what it truly wants."

They talked awhile longer until Carroll announced time was up. "Would you like to make another appointment?"

"Can I see how things go this week?" Pam said.

"Of course. Good luck to you. I'll have to come down to the village and walk your beautiful garden. Frankie says it's extraordinary."

"Please do, anytime." Pam hugged her. Carroll Ranglund really knew how to hug.

*****

After the firing-Murph incident, Sandy had mostly kept his temper in check, concentrating on work and summer bookings. Lolly consented to let him take Maisie for a week's vacation to Spruce Point in Maine. They had a wonderful time hiking the trails, swimming, canoeing, and sitting around the campfire every night for s'mores. He was propositioned by women day and night at the resort and frequently at the club. Ordinarily, he'd have hooked up with a few. Then there were his former girlfriends, who were everywhere, but all he could think about was Pam. The curve of her hips, her sweet smile, her skin as soft as a newborn child's. Most of all, he missed talking with her and sitting beside her, arms touching, hands entwined.

The night after he returned from vacation, he was sitting at the far end of the main bar when Murph found him. "Hey, boss, why don't we invite a couple of ladies for an afterhours drink tonight? There's a lot of 'em, and they're hot."

"What would Sasha have to say about that?" Sandy asked, referring to Murph's live-in girlfriend.

"She's away visiting her sister on the Vineyard."

"Thanks, but I've gotta get home."

"Bullshit."

"I just don't feel like it, Murph. Leave it alone."

"She's not comin' back, man. You gotta move on."

"Didn't I just say to leave it?" Sandy turned away and headed for the kitchen just as a blonde headed his way.

"Evenin'," Murph said. "Can I get you something?"

"Your boss. I've been trying to talk to him all night."

"He's off the market at the moment, but I'm not."

She gave him a sharp look. "What are you talking about? I'm married, see?" She held up her left hand to reveal a wedding band and another ring with an enormous diamond. "This is business."

"Well, he seldom conducts business while the bands are playing. Would you want to make an appointment?"

"Oh, for heaven's sake. Give him this and tell him to meet me on the deck in five minutes." She handed Murph her business card and walked away. He glanced down at the card. *Cady Promotions. Elizabeth Cady, owner.*

Murph whistled under his breath, heading for the kitchen. He found Sandy in the small back office doing paperwork. He never did paperwork in the evenings. "Hey, boss, guess who's in the audience?"

"Not this again."

"Elizabeth Cady. Ring a bell?"

Sandy gazed up. "The promoter?"

"The very one, and she wants you to meet her on the deck in five."

Sandy shook his head. "Yeah, right."

"It's not what you think. She's married."

"When's that ever stopped anyone?"

"I don't think she's hitting on you," Murph said. "Go on. See what she wants."

"Fine." Sandy grabbed Cady's business card and slammed out of the kitchen.

"I have a good mind to call Pam Morgan and pay her to take him back," Murph said to the cook. "This is getting really old."

Sandy stepped onto the packed deck, scanning the crowd. A tall blonde stood near the far railing sipping a Cosmo. He headed toward her and was interrupted several times by regulars wanting to say hello. When he finally reached her, Cady's glass was empty. "You're a popular guy, Mr. Rodriguez."

"Sandy, please."

"Elizabeth Cady." She gave him a firm handshake. "Shall we walk to the end of the dock where it's quieter?"

"Whatever," he said, ushering her through the crowd to the long wooden dock.

When they reached the end, she sat on one of the benches, patting the seat beside her.

"What's this about?" he asked, recognizing a come-hither gesture when he saw it.

"I'm not trying to get you into bed, if you're thinking like your obtuse manager."

"So what can I do for you?" She was a big woman, all curves, dressed to the nines in designer jeans and a buttery red leather jacket. Her shoulder-length blonde hair framed an angular, but attractive face. Older than she looked at first glance, her makeup was expertly applied.

"It's what I can do for you, Sandy dear. We're been watching you and the club for some time."

"Excuse me?"

"There isn't much in the East Coast music scene we don't keep an eye on."

"Should I be flattered?"

She shrugged. "That's your call, honey. I'm here to make you an offer."

"I'm not interested in selling the club."

"You might be once you hear what I have to say. Cady is trying to consolidate the venues we own while adding a few we think have potential. Then we can block groups for a circuit, coordinate publicity, and, of course, attract bigger names. Our company is publicly traded, so you could still be a major stockholder if you so choose."

"Listen, Ms. Cady. I'm flattered, truly, but I built this place from nothing. We're doing well, and I have great employees who've been with me since the beginning."

"And who could stay on. You too, if you wanted to have a role."

He shook his head. "Not interested."

She smiled, handing him an envelope. "All I ask is that you think about it. The offer's in there, but terms, roles, employees, and all are all negotiable. Open it at home and give it some thought. My card's in there if you have questions."

"Okay."

She held up her empty glass. "Now *I* need a refill. I'll be in touch."

"Tell the bartender it's on me," he said, watching as she sashayed down the dock and disappeared into the crowd. He slipped the envelope into his back pocket and followed, but by the time he got inside, Elizabeth Cady had disappeared.

Murph spied him near the bar and rushed over. "What'd she want?"

"To buy the club."

"No!" Murph's eyes were big as saucers.

"Don't worry, I said no."

"Was it a good offer?"

"Don't know. Haven't looked at it. I'll let you know tomorrow. I'm gonna head home. You okay to close up?"

"Got it," Murph said.

"Don't worry. Your job's secure," Sandy said, patting him on the shoulder.

CHAPTER 33

At home, weary and discouraged, Sandy grabbed a beer, then went out to the deck to enjoy the late evening. A beautiful night, the crescent-moon sky was blanketed with stars. He leaned back and closed his eyes. *Something's gotta change. I can't keep going on like this.* Then he remembered the envelope in his back pocket. He reached back, flipping on the porch light, then pulled out Elizabeth Cady's offer.

When he read the amount, he shot out of the glider, going inside where the light was better, assuming he had misread the amount. Cady Promotions was offering him six and a half million for Sandy's. This included the two-acre waterfront property and the club. His parents had bought the land almost forty years ago, intending to build a restaurant on the bluffs. Then the Grille had taken off in town, and they deeded it over to their twenty-one-year-old with the big dreams and singular vision. In the past two decades, waterfront property had become priceless.

Sandy shook his head. By rights, any profits should be split with his parents. But did he even want to sell? *Geez, talk about a monkey wrench my life. First Pam Morgan, now this.* He tossed the offer on the kitchen counter and decided it was time for bed.

*****

Pam saw three clients at the new building, then strolled across the street to the garden. She loved their new office space, and not only because of its location. It was light and airy, the sun streaming in. She had taken care to choose comfortable furnishings, and the space was her own. She had brought a salad, which she opened once seated in a shady spot near the rear of the garden. There were only a few empty plots left now, a source of pride and satisfaction to her. A few gardeners worked their plots, and two volunteers watered and raked as she watched, a smile on her face.

"What a huge accomplishment. You must feel so great about this," a voice said beside her. She turned to find Lolly LaSalle standing over her.

Pam nodded. "Yes, our mother would have loved it."

"Everyone loves it. It's been such a wonderful addition to the village." Like her mother, Lolly had a flamboyance about her. Bright violet eyes and shoulder-length raven hair, all curves compared to Pam's assessment of herself as flat and skinny. *What a difference it must have been for him to hold me after her.* Lolly looked better than she had the last time they'd met. Rested and calm. "In fact," she went on, "Mom was talking about expanding it next year, if there's a need."

"Really?" Pam said, surprised at the news and at the other's friendliness.

"Yup."

"I'm afraid I wolfed down my salad, but I have plenty of iced tea in this thermos. Would you like some?"

"No, thanks. I just ate. Mind if I sit a few minutes?"

Pam gazed up wide-eyed. "Of course." She moved her lunch bag to the ground beside her.

"So how's life?" Lolly asked, staring straight ahead.

"Busy."

"Are you and Sandy doing well?"

Pam turned to stare at her. *Could she really not know?* "I haven't seen Sandy for weeks."

"That's a shock. I thought after seeing you at the wedding, you'd be married or engaged by now."

"We're not together, Lolly."

"Why not?"

"Well, for one thing, I didn't want to do anything to jeopardize his relationship with your daughter."

"Maisie? They just got back from a really fun vacation. Why would you think that?"

"Because… I mean… The lawsuit and all."

Lolly waved her hand. "Oh, that. That was just me and one last attempt to hold on. Sandy and I don't belong together. Never did. It was easy for me to blame him when he cheated, but I drove him away."

"Why?"

"I didn't love him."

"Why did you marry him, then?"

Lolly smiled. "I got pregnant. And at that point in my life, I'd have done anything to break free of my mother. Now look where I ended up. Right back under her thumb."

"Does Sandy know all that?"

Lolly shook her head. "After Maisie was born, I shut down completely. Major postpartum depression. I locked him out of our bedroom for over a year. Wouldn't let him touch me, never mind anything else."

"Then why did you care if he started seeing someone else?"

"Honestly, I didn't. I was actually relieved he didn't need me for sex or intimacy. But this is a small town. I had to pretend to be wronged when we decided to divorce."

"Why?"

"'Cause I'm a bitch."

"What's changed now?"

"Well, for one, I'm seeing a great therapist. She's in Southport. I'm also taking meds to help the depression."

"Good therapists are such a gift," Pam said.

Lolly nodded. "I saw a bunch of bad therapists before her. Of course, I couldn't consult our resident therapist as she's one of Sandy's former girlfriends. Then there's you, which would have been very awkward."

Pam smiled. "Well, I'm glad you found someone. Frankie recommended a great person to me in Bayport."

"Lemme guess—Carroll?"

Pam nodded.

"I didn't try her because—again—too close for comfort."

They sat quietly, observing the activity in the garden for a few minutes until Lolly said, "So when are you going back to him?"

"Sandy?"

Lolly nodded, drawing a circle with a stick on the ground in front of her. "Who do you think?"

"It might be a little late for us now."

"That's got to be the dumbest thing I've ever heard anyone say."

"I'm not great at messy situations."

"Then get ready to live like a hermit for the rest of your life. I can tell you from experience, it sucks."

"You really wouldn't mind if we were dating?"

"Would I be here talking to you if I did?"

Pam smiled. "Well, time will tell, I guess."

"Better not let too much time elapse. My spies told me a blonde was all over him at the club last night." Lolly stood up, tossing her stick in a nearby compost pile. "I leave you to your meditation."

"Thanks, Lolly. And please tell your mom I'd love to consider expanding the garden next summer, if she's serious."

"Will do."

As Lolly passed through the arbor out of the garden, Pam leaned back, not sure what to think about the encounter. One thing was certain. She wanted to see Sandy, but how?

She needed a few things in town, so she left her car in the garden lot and walked the half mile to Main Street. She was headed for Village Books when she ran right into Sandy coming out of the Grille. She grabbed his shoulders to steady herself, then stepped back. He had grasped hold of her waist, but reluctantly released her. "Hey."

"So sorry. My mind was a million miles away," she said.

"Mine too. Clearly. How are you?"

"Fine. You?"

"Okay."

An awkward silence fell over them as people passed by. Finally she said, "Sandy I… I would like to… I mean, do you ride horses?"

"Excuse me?"

"Do you ride?"

"Not very well."

"Me either, but would you like to take a ride sometime?"

Puzzled, he studied her. Something had shifted in her demeanor. She seemed less guarded, more open. His mind was swimming with the Cady Promotions business and the conversation he'd just had with his parents, but he heard himself say, "Sure. Why not?"

"Tomorrow afternoon? Around three?"

"Works for me. Where?"

"Can you meet me at the farm? I'll double-check to make sure the two stable horses will be free then. If they're not, I'll call you."

"Great. See you then."

As Pam hurried into the bookstore, he grinned. *Forget the six and a half million. This is a hell of a lot more exciting.*

CHAPTER 34

The two sisters stood in the barn, sunlight pouring in. Weezie grinned as she extracted something from her back pocket. "Don't s'pose you'll be needing these on your ride, will you?"

Pam turned bright red as she spied her panties. "Where did you…?"

"Dennis found them when he was cleaning stalls and needed fresh hay," she said, referring to Dennis Farrell, the assistant farm manager. "I said they weren't mine, but I'd check around with my lady friends."

Pam frowned. "Then why are you waving them in my face?"

"Because I recognized them from our trip to that fancy lingerie shop before Lucy and Dad's wedding. Remember you just had to have them?"

"Ha-ha, now give them to me." Pam reached forward and snatched them out of her hand.

"Won't ask how they got in the hayloft or when," her sister said, dark brown eyes dancing with mischief as Pam stuffed the panties into the side pocket of her pack.

"Good, 'cause I'm not telling you. Now, we all set here?"

Weezie tightened Crackers's saddle, giving Pam a look. "Are you sure about this, sis? I mean, you haven't ridden a horse since you got here, and it was a while ago in Maine."

"I'll be fine. We'll go slow, and the trail around the village is easy."

"Except near Land's End where it's really uneven. Be careful through there. No crazy gallops or—"

Pam patted Sheba's flank. "I can guarantee that I will not be doing any crazy galloping anywhere."

"Who's riding this guy?" Weezie asked, nuzzling Crackers's nose.

"I thought Sandy, but what do you think?"

"Whoever's the steadier rider."

"We'll discuss it. Now, don't hover. He'll be here soon."

"I'm in the barn if you need me," Weezie said, wrapping the horse's lead around the fence post next to Sheba.

As Sandy drove in and parked by the farmhouse, Kyle Morgan was just coming out of the barn, shirtsleeves rolled up, medical bag under his arm. "Hey!" he called. "What brings you over here?"

"Riding. With Pam."

Kyle grinned. "You got a good day for it. Nice breeze, not too hot."

"What are you here for?"

"Just routine check-ups, and they've discovered that one of the recent acquisitions is pregnant."

"One of the thoroughbreds?"

Kyle shook his head. "Nah. They haven't had much luck in the thoroughbred department. Finding horses with great potential is hard for a new stable. No, it's one of the wild ones. Nellie, a pretty pinto they brought in from Nevada. Her belly was swollen, and they thought it was bloat or starvation, but she's with foal. It'll be the first for the mustangs here."

"Is that a good thing?"

Kyle wiped his forehead. "If you want more horses it is. Have a great ride. You going on the peninsula trail?"

"Yup."

"I might catch a glimpse of you out at Land's End. That's where I'm headed now."

"You're a busy doc, huh?"

Kyle laughed. "No rest for the wicked, but I love it. I spend mornings in the office and most afternoons doing house calls. It's a perfect balance, and who wouldn't want to cruise around this beautiful area every day?"

Sandy nodded. "I hear you there. I'd better get down to the stables. I'll look for you out at the Point."

"See ya." The young vet turned away and headed for his truck.

Sandy strolled down the short path from the farmhouse to the barn, where he met Richard Morgan. "Afternoon, son. I hear you're goin' out for a ride."

"Hey, sir. Yup, that's the plan."

"Well, my little firecracker's got the horses all saddled up. Love to come along and wave you off, but I'm expecting a wine broker, and I've got to get to the vineyard."

"How's it going down there?"

Richard grinned, the same Morgan smile he'd just seen on Kyle. "It's a work in progress. Come down sometime. Wolfie'd love to give you a tour. Enjoy your ride." Richard patted him on the shoulder and hurried off.

When he rounded the barn, Sandy spied Pam petting a chestnut Morgan as she whispered softly. A tall American paint horse stood beside them, nickering, no doubt waiting for attention as well. Pam was dressed in jeans and a blue plaid flannel shirt hanging loose over her white T-shirt. Even in her baggy apparel, her soft curves sent his libido into overdrive, and he felt himself grow hard. *Whoa, boy. It'll be a long ride if you don't rein yourself in!*

Pam spied him and waved. "Hi, we're all set. I have snacks in my saddle bag."

"Great." As he reached her, he planted a chaste kiss on her cheek. "Good to see you."

Pam gave him a shy smile. "You too."

*****

They were a few miles along and had just connected to the eighteen-mile bridle path that ringed the peninsula. As her western cousins were fond of saying, there's nothing like a man on a horse, Pam thought as she followed Sandy and Crackers. The expression was often "a man in a Stetson," but her man was wearing baseball cap. Pam noticed every movement, the curve of his shoulders, the arch of his back, and that amazing ass. Despite his claims to being an amateur, he sat confidently and comfortably in the saddle.

When she had told him that Crackers needed a steady rider, he hadn't hesitated and had mounted the horse in one fluid motion. Her ascent onto Sheba had been a little less graceful, but she'd managed it without falling or embarrassing herself. What she'd really wanted to do was drag him into the barn and make wild, crazy love in the hayloft. His smile was enough to dampen her panties.

As the trail widened, he reined Crackers in, waiting for Sheba to come alongside. "Great day for it."

"Yes."

"Thanks for this. I haven't ridden in ages, and it feels good. I'm glad to see you. I've missed you."

"I've missed you too. Let's keep going a little ways. Weezie says there's a really nice overlook just after Land's End. We can stop there."

"You want to lead?"

"No, you go ahead. Weezie also says the next few miles, the ground gets a little uneven, so rein Crackers firmly."

He smiled. "I know exactly where she means. I've tripped many a time while running or nearly crashed my bike. You look beautiful on a horse, by the way."

Pam blushed. "Thanks. If I can only stay on. You look pretty great yourself, and I think you were downplaying your riding prowess."

"Don't speak yet," he said, nudging Crackers forward. "We've got sixteen or so miles to go."

CHAPTER 35

As they passed Land's End, Sandy spied Kyle's truck parked by the barn, but no one was about except some workers in one of the far fields. They were riding side by side at that point, and he said, "He's a great guy, your cousin the vet."

"Yes, we love him and we love Harriet too. It's just amazing that they got together and now they're back here."

"Sounds like quite a place, their valley. I'm surprised they chose to come back."

"He came for Harriet so she could keep her job and be near her family, but Kyle loves the East Coast. He went to college back here."

"Oh?"

"Tufts. I think that was it. He has a lot of East Coast friends, and they spent vacations on Cape Cod and the Vineyard. He was happy to come back."

"Lucky us. My parents worship their cats and dogs. They're in love with Dr. Kyle."

She smiled, smoothing strands of hair from her face. "Here we are."

The horses climbed a short rise to a grassy knoll ringed on three sides by thick stands of rosa rugosa, sweet peas, and golden rod. The choppy green blue waters of the bay stretched out in front of them. "This is a cool place," he said, dismounting.

"Lovely," she said, also dismounting and slipping the pack from Sheba's flank. She had also brought a small blanket, which she handed to him.

Sandy spread the blanket on the grass near the edge of the clearing, affording them a beautiful view of the bay. He watched her lay out cheese, crackers, and olives. Then she pulled a bottle of Merlot and two plastic cups from the pack. "I thought red was safer since I couldn't keep it cool. Sorry about the plastic."

"It's perfect," he said, taking the bottle and corkscrew and deftly uncorking it.

Wine in hand, they sat gazing out at the water for several minutes. This was her party, and Sandy had decided to let her take the lead, but she didn't seem to be in any hurry. Finally, he said, "I was surprised to get your call. Happy, but surprised."

Still staring outward, she nodded. "Yes."

"Was there something on your mind?"

"Sort of… I mean, I've been thinking."

"And?"

Pam set down her cup and turned her body to face him. "I had a visit from Lolly yesterday. Just before I ran into you."

"Uh-oh."

Pam put up her hands. "No, it was fine. Strange and surprising, but fine. She wanted to… Well, I'm not sure what she wanted, but in the course of the conversation, she told me she'd let go."

"Of?"

"I guess of any hope of you and her. She was surprised that you and I weren't seeing each other."

Sandy's eyes flashed fire. "So this whole thing was orchestrated by my ex? She gave you permission to be with me, and now it's okay?"

"No, no, it isn't like that at all."

"Pam, I've been going crazy missing you these past few weeks. Now you're telling me Lolly's given us permission to date, so it's okay?"

"Please, Sandy. It's not like that at all. I won't lie and say that the messiness of Lolly and her threats to keep you and Maisie apart weren't upsetting. They were. But I was scared of so many things. Of losing my heart to someone who does have a bit of a reputation."

Sandy stood, throwing the dregs of his wine on the grass as he began pacing back and forth. The horses grazed nearby. They seemed to pick up on his agitation and began whinnying and stomping their hooves. Pam watched for several minutes, unable to move. Finally, she gathered the food and wine bottle, stuffed it in the pack, and stood to fold the blanket.

When he noticed her, he said, "What are you doing?"

"Looks like we'd better keep going. We still have almost twelve miles to get back to the farm."

He paused, staring at her, his expression unreadable. "You're probably right. I'd like to talk about this sometime, but not now. I've got a lot on my mind. I'm sorry."

Pam fought back tears as she secured the pack and hopped up on Sheba. Her heart felt like it had been ripped from her chest. Without a word, she started off on the lower trail that led by the village and up into the countryside at the opposite end of town. Sandy followed, but she never looked back. It seemed like hours before the farmhouse and barns of Morgan's Fire came into view. Pam was sore and tired as she guided Sheba past the barn. Dennis Farrell, the assistant trainer, was there with two other guys they'd hired for the summer. "Evening, folks. Can we take those horses for you?"

"Thanks, Dennis, that'd be great," Pam said, slipping off Sheba. She grabbed the pack and waited until Sandy had dismounted and given Crackers over to Dennis.

Sandy had parked by the farmhouse, but her car was parked alongside the barn.

He followed her to the Subaru, where she turned to face him. "You're angry."

"I am. I also know that I'm acting like an asshole, but I can't talk about this right now."

She reached out and touched his arm, her whole being crying out for him. "Please don't be angry with Lolly. It wasn't calculated. In fact, I think she spotted me in the garden and was actually trying to be friendly."

He smiled, leaning down, kissing her softly. "I need to sort through some things."

"Is this how you break up with people?" she asked, breathless after the kiss.

"Hardly. I'm in love with you. I couldn't break up with you if I wanted to."

"Then please talk to me."

"I can't. I've got to meet someone."

"The blonde?" Pam blushed, horrified at what had slipped out of her mouth. "I'm sorry. That was stupid."

He studied her curiously, then whistled. "This fricking town. No secrets. Don't worry about the blonde. It's not what you think." He kissed her forehead. "Okay if I call you?"

She nodded, then slipped into the car. As she drove off, he turned and headed back to the farmhouse.

Richard and Lucy were on the porch having a cocktail, and he called to Sandy. "Did I just see Pam go by? How was the ride?"

"Great. Pretty day, and I didn't fall off, so that's something."

"How 'bout a drink?" Richard asked.

"Thanks, but I've got an appointment. Enjoy." He nodded to Lucy, then headed for his truck.

"Trouble in Paradise, I think," Lucy said, turning to her husband.

Richard shook his head. "I think you may be right, sweetheart. Always something around here, isn't it?"

CHAPTER 36

Elizabeth Cady perched on one of the barstools, sipping iced tea, a folder of papers in front of her. Tortoiseshell reading glasses were perched at the end of her nose, and she was dressed in tailored linen capris and a sleeveless white linen top. Neither garment had a wrinkle, her hair was perfectly coifed, and her jewelry understated and expensive. Murph had been watching her from the kitchen, intrigued by this exotic foreigner. *Where the hell is the boss?* He was just about to head out to refresh her tea when Sandy stepped into the kitchen.

"Hey, it's about time! Ms. Devil Wears Prada's been waiting on you for half an hour."

Sandy consulted his watch. "We weren't scheduled to meet until now. I can't help it if she's early."

"So?"

"So what?"

"Was it a good offer?"

"Yup."

"What're you gonna do?"

"Nothing today. I want to get some specifics, then I'll talk everything over with you, my folks, and the staff. If it doesn't work for everyone, it's not happening. And before you ask, I'm not sure it works for me. Sit tight, man. And bring me a seltzer, would you?"

He greeted Elizabeth Cady with a firm handshake. "Sorry to keep you waiting."

"No worries. I'm early. I wanted to get the feel of the place empty."

"Won't be for long."

"So what did you think? Are you ready to let Cady Promotions take this place to the next level and make you a huge pile of money in the process?"

"Not yet. I have a bunch of questions, then I plan to take it back to my employees. If it doesn't work for them, it's no deal. As I just told my manager, I'm not yet sure it even works for me, but I'm willing to talk."

They spent an hour going over details, mostly about what would happen to the staff in a buyout. As people started trickling into the club, she snapped her folder shut and said, "I'll leave you to it. I'm flying to California in the morning, but I'll be back the end of the week. Shall we set up a meet for Saturday?"

*****

Lemon Grass, the jazz group, had just started its second set when Sandy excused himself and went out to the parking lot. People milled around, drinks in hand, smoking, mostly cigarettes, but he caught whiffs of marijuana as well. The club had a strict no-smoking rule, even on the deck, so the diehard smokers had only the parking lot for their habit.

Ignoring his patrons, Sandy unlocked the truck and slipped into the cab, pulling out his cell phone. She answered on the second ring. "Hey," he said. "How are you?"

Her voice registered surprise as Pam said, "Fine…confused. Okay, I guess."

"Well, I'm not, and I'm sorry. The mention of Lolly's interference in all this pushed a button, and I acted like a horse's ass. I wanted to apologize."

"We both have stuff, but let's leave it behind. Okay?"

"Works for me. Listen, where are you?"

"At home."

"Do you know Sebring Park?"

"Yes. It's near your club, isn't it?"

"Wanna meet me there for a nightcap? If you don't, that's okay. I can—"

"I'd love to. When?"

"Half an hour?"

"I'll be there."

*****

When Pam got out of her car, he was seated on a bench in the shadows, shielded from the road and the seawall by huge stands of shrubbery. As she crossed the space between them, he stood and opened his arms. "Oh, baby, I've missed you." He captured her lips for a deep kiss, tongue curled round hers as his hands moved up and down the body he loved more than life itself.

Pam felt his erection, impossibly big against her, and she lost all reason, a delicious shiver of wanting running through her as her pulse quickened and she moaned. His hands were underneath her jersey, releasing her round soft breasts from her bra, squeezing, teasing, stroking until her nipples were rock hard and her first orgasm swept over her, leaving her limp in his arms yet wanting more.

"I love you," he whispered as his expert hands divested her of jeans and panties and he quickly shed his own.

"I love you too," she moaned. "More than I could ever say."

"You ready for me, baby?"

"What do you think?" Her fingers raked through his thick hair, begging him to take her.

Sandy slipped on a condom, then slid his fingers up her thigh to her moist, warm center, finding her clit and sending her off the deep end again. "Oh oh oh," she moaned. "Please, Sandy. Please!"

"Okay, my sweet girl. I know what you want," he said, lifting her, wrapping her legs around his waist as he eased back down on the backless bench, allowing her legs to fall behind them as he plunged into her. Hard.

Pam gasped and then reared up, digging her fingers into his shoulders. As she rammed down on him, she urged him to go deeper. He held on as long as he could, then, as she screamed in climax, he let go in a thunderous, roaring release.

As they sat limp and sated in each other's arms, he whispered, "Geez, baby. Wow. I wasn't sure how this evening was gonna go, but never in my wildest dreams did I imagine this."

Pam smiled, kissing his neck as she moved above him, pleased to feel him grow inside her. "I guess that's what absence does to us."

"If you say so, baby."

She groaned as he slipped out of her warm depths and slipped on another condom. For a second he held her above him. "Ready sweetie?"

Pam nodded and he brought her down onto him and they began again, this time more slowly and languidly, their simultaneous orgasm all breath and touching.

As they rested wrapped around each other, he kissed her shoulder. "Sorry, baby, but I've gotta get back. Want to come with me?"

As they moved apart and began dressing, she said, "Thanks, but I think I'll head home. You're welcome to come to my house after work."

"Tempting as that is, let's plan something for tomorrow. I'm gonna be here till the wee hours 'cause it's my turn to close, and this band does a million encores."

"Call me?" she said, fully dressed now, standing in front of him.

"I will. Probably not till midday."

"Night," she said, still shocked at the past hour's turn of events.

"Night my love," he said, kissing her deeply, arms wrapping her in a cocoon of heat.

As he released her, Pam felt a shiver run up her spine and wondered if she should go back to the club. After the past hour, she never wanted to leave him. Finally, she drew back and hurried to the car. "See you tomorrow, then?"

"Count on it."

Chapter 37

As Pam drove home, every fiber of her being was on fire. She hadn't known what to expect at Sebring Park, but never in her craziest dreams had she envisioned *that*!

When she arrived at her house, she sat in the car for a few minutes, head resting on the steering wheel, collecting herself, wondering if Sebring Park had made things better or worse. It was crazy!

A tapping on her window roused her. Startled, she looked up to find Frankie Brown. "You okay, dear?"

Embarrassed, Pam hopped out of the car. "Hi, Frankie. You're out late."

"Darn Yarners meeting. We were having so much fun, we lost track of time. Want to come in for some tea or a nightcap?"

"Don't you want to go to bed?"

"Not when I can have a cup of chamomile with my neighbor. Come on. I have stronger things too."

Pam followed her through the house that reflected its hobbit-like outside. A rabbit warren of rooms filled with bric-a-brac, knickknacks, artwork, and shelves of books. "Wow, you have a lot of collections," she said as they reached the kitchen, every shelf covered with curios and an odd assortment of china.

"It's a disease. One of these days, I'm going to hire someone to come and cart it all away," Frankie said as she put the kettle on.

"Why?"

"It becomes oppressive. Would you like tea or a drink? I have soft drinks, juice, and water too."

"Tea would be great, and chamomile sounds perfect."

"Looks like you had a fun evening," Frankie said, pulling a box of tea bags from the cupboard.

Pam gazed down and was mortified to see that her blouse was misbuttoned and her jeans partially unzipped. Giving up all pretense, she zipped up and began rebuttoning her blouse. "You could say that."

"Those are my favorite kind," Frankie said, grinning broadly. "Do you take anything in your tea?"

"A little honey if you have it. Thanks."

They took their mugs out to the back porch and sat side by side in wicker chairs, their worn cushions lumpy but soft.

"So how do you like village life?" Frankie asked after a few minutes of silence.

"I love it. I mean, it takes a bit of getting used to, everyone knowing your business and all, but our town in Maine wasn't that different."

Intense blue eyes gazed at her, and Pam was struck by the beauty she saw in the tall sixty-something woman with curly salt-and-pepper hair. "The garden's wonderful. Such an asset. I've been meaning to ask if there are any plots left."

"Yes, at least five I think. Are you interested?"

"Only if no one else wants them. I can always wait until Mavis's expansion."

"You know about that?"

"She was full of it tonight."

"We haven't even spoken."

Frankie smiled. "Small town."

"Did she say she was going solo or joining with the current garden?"

"I believe she intends to join forces. I'm sure she'll contact you soon. Wedding season's in high gear, so I'm guessing she's in the 'all talk, no action' phase right now."

"Just as well. Gearing up for an expansion would be a lot right now."

"Rosa mentioned you tonight."

Pam's heart sank. "Oh?"

"Says you're dating her son."

"Sort of."

"I've always liked the lad. I wonder what he'll do when the club's sold."

"Excuse me?"

"Sorry, I assumed you knew. We have no secrets at the Yarners, and we protect each other's secrets, so I probably shouldn't have spoken."

"Well, now you have," Pam said, setting down her mug. "Who's buying the club?"

"Some big promoter. Sandy's parents were flabbergasted at the sum. Waterfront property has gone crazy the past decade. It says a lot about their son that he came right to them and wanted to share the profit. Of course, they refused."

"Why *would* he offer to share? Were they part owners?"

"No, but it was originally their land. They had planned to turn the old building into a restaurant but then started the Grille and decided one business was enough. They deeded it over to Sandy. Don't know if money changed hands, but if it did, it wasn't much."

"Huh," Pam said. Not knowing what else to say, she changed the subject. "Have you always lived here, Frankie?"

"About thirty years, but like my dear friend Helen Winthrop, I summered here at first."

"Where were you before that?"

"Boston."

"Boston, really? You don't seem like a city girl."

"But my husband was, and I was in love. When we divorced, I bought this little place—for a song I might add—and have been here ever since."

"Do you have kids?"

"Only the ones I've adopted as a Darn Yarner. I consider all Yarner offspring as my nieces and nephews. I'm particularly close to your stepmother and her sisters."

"Lucky for them. I hope this isn't too personal, but did you date after your divorce?"

Frankie chuckled. "I'm still dating. I do the online thing off and on and sometimes have blind dates through friends."

"Really?"

"Not much luck, I'm afraid, although I've met lots of nice people. Leonard kind of poisoned the well. My ex. I was crazy about him. I've never found anyone like him."

"Are you… I mean, do you stay in touch?"

"Occasionally. He's a very prominent architect. Has designed some of the most iconic buildings in the country, so he travels a lot."

"Is his name Brown?"

"No, Paltz. Leonard Paltz. You can google him and find millions of links."

Frankie was smiling, but her eyes betrayed a sadness in their azure depths. "I hope I wasn't prying."

"Never."

Pam stood and stretched. "I'd better get to bed and let you do the same. Thanks for the tea."

"Anytime. I love the company. I've been meaning to get you over to dinner, so we'll plan something soon."

"I'd love that."

"And good luck with your guy," Frankie said as Pam set her mug on the counter and turned to go.

"Thanks. Night."

CHAPTER 38

Sandy woke midmorning and rubbed sleep from his eyes. In truth, he hadn't slept much, churning over what he needed to say to his staff today. He'd called a meeting for noon. Even more importantly there was Pam. He thought for a while, then grinned. He punched in her number. "Hey, baby," he said. "How're you doing?"

"Great."

"Listen I've got some things to take care of, but I really want to see you. What's your day like?"

"I've got clients till about one, then I'll head over to the garden for an hour or two."

"Can you meet me at Sebring Park? It'll be broad daylight, so you're safe. No funny business."

"Funny business? Is that what last night was?"

"And a whole lot more. But I want to talk to you, and I don't want to do it in a restaurant or place with people around. I mean, after, we can get something to eat if you like."

"What time?"

"You tell me. Three? Four?"

"Let's say four in case the garden's busy. It's such a beautiful day, a lot of people may be there."

"Four it is. See you." He rang off and tossed the phone on the bed on his way to the shower.

After calling and ordering bunch of food from the Café, he was out the door fifteen minutes later. He headed into town but had one stop to make before he collected the Café order. Mission accomplished, he strolled down Main Street, a huge grin on his face. His brother Vincent was just going into work at the Grille, and the brothers met outside their parents' restaurant.

"Hey, bro, you look like a happy camper," Vincent said.

"That's 'cause I am."

"That's good, 'cause we're all tired of seeing your moping about."

"Ha-ha."

"Your good mood wouldn't have anything to do with Elizabeth Cady, would it?"

"So Mom and Dad told you?"

"Yup. Congrats. You gonna take it?"

"Still thinking."

"About what? You'd be the richest man in town."

Sandy smiled. "I think Richard Morgan has me beat on that score. Listen, are you guys all right with this? I mean, Mom and Dad sold me that land for a song."

"Can't speak for the rest of 'em, but I'm thrilled for you, man. It's not like any of us couldn't have bid on that property. It was your vision. You built Sandy's to what it is today. It's your capital she's buying."

"Let's be honest. The club's doing well, but the value is the land. You can't tell me Cady doesn't plan to develop it."

"Relax. It's your day. We'll all be cool with it."

"Thanks, Vin."

"Hey, did I see you coming out of Perkins Jewelry?"

"Yeah, my sunglasses broke, and he's the only person in town that carries Ray-Ban."

Vincent grinned. "Uh-huh. Where are these alleged glasses?"

"He had to order them."

"I see. Well, gotta get to work. Have a good one, and good luck with your decision, although from where I'm sitting, it's a no-brainer."

Sandy patted his shoulder. "Thanks. See you around."

*****

The meeting with his staff went well. He made it clear that nothing would change except ownership. Murph, if he chose, could continue as manager, and they would bring in someone from Cady to work alongside him. After lunch, he sat down with Murph to talk further.

"So you're going ahead with it, boss?"

"Not if you're not cool with it."

"Does your agreement with Cady specify that I have to stay?"

"Of course not. You're free to do whatever you want. Always have been, always will be."

"Okay."

"Why, are you thinking you want to try something different?" Sandy asked, gazing at his friend and colleague.

"Not necessarily. Just want to keep my options open."

"Good, 'cause if I dream up some new venture, I'll be trying to bring you onboard."

Murph smiled. "A venture better than Sandy's? Always knew you are a miracle worker. You gonna be here tonight?"

"Later. You okay opening up?"

"Yup. Big plans?"

"Kind of." Sandy checked his watch. It was three forty-five. "Listen, Murph, I've gotta go. See you around nine. You okay introducing the guys?"

"If Delaney and Hall aren't used to me by now, they'd better get used to me. Go! I'll see you when I see you."

CHAPTER 39

This time, Pam was waiting for him. When he drove in, several families were picnicking on the grass nearby. She sat on a bench overlooking the sea. He waved, and she returned the gesture as he strolled toward her.

He grinned, spreading his arms, gesturing to their surroundings. "See, nice and public, no funny business. You look beautiful in the sunlight."

She arched one eyebrow, smiling at him. "Thanks. I am kind of disappointed about no funny business."

"We can get to that later. That skimpy dress will make things very easy. Right now, I want to talk."

"Skimpy? This is one of my favorite summer dresses."

"Well, you look sexy as hell in it."

Public place, public place, Pam mused, thinking things could get out of hand in a heartbeat. "I hear congratulations are in order," she said as he sat beside her. He looked tired, but gorgeous as always in jeans and a gray T-shirt that hugged his muscular chest. Had they been alone, she would have happily dug her fingers into that chest and begged him to make love to her.

Sandy smacked his head. "Should have known. Small town. Who told you?"

She smiled. "Frankie."

"Frankie! How the hell did she know?"

"Apparently, it was a hot topic at last night's Darn Yarners."

"Geez. I forget that those broads tell each other everything. They have some secret code or something."

"Broads?"

"Women, ladies, whatever. I do want to tell you about the offer to buy the club, but there's something else first."

"Oh? Is everything okay?"

"More than okay. Listen, baby, I know you're kind of an old-fashioned girl." He slipped off the bench and got down on one knee.

Pam clapped her hand over her mouth, eyes wide.

He grinned. "Pam Morgan, as I hope is obvious, I'm crazy in love with you. I've gotten to the place in my life where I cannot imagine another day without you. Every part of my body aches for you day and all night. I'm asking…no, begging you to put me out of my misery and be my wife. Will you marry me?" He opened a tiny black velvet box to revealed a very large diamond ring.

Stunned, she gazed down, first at the ring, then into his dark eyes. "It's so beautiful. Are you sure?"

"Would I be down on my knees begging if I wasn't? If you need time, just say so, but please don't say no right now. Give it some thought and—"

"Yes."

"Yes, you'll give it some thought?" He smiled, a soft loving smile that went straight to her heart.

"Yes, I'll marry you, Sandy Rodriguez. I love you so much, and I don't want to spend another day without you either." She wrapped her arms around his neck, leaning down to kiss him.

"See what I mean about that dress?" he said.

"Come up here and give me a proper kiss," she said. "Then let's go home. I don't care which home as long as we're together."

"You got it, baby," he said, then swept her off the bench and into his arms.

"Not in front of the kids," she whispered as children's voices sounded nearby.

"I love you, and I don't care if the whole world knows. I give the village grapevine thirty minutes, and then everyone'll be up to speed. Now, can we try this ring on? If you don't like it, we can shop for another."

"I love it, and I love you," Pam said as he slipped the ring on her finger. Not surprisingly, it fit perfectly.

Please read on for sample chapters of **Rich's Dilemma**, book four in the **Morgan's Fire** series!

I am so excited to bring you a sneak preview of book four in the Morgan's Fire series which debuts in 2020. This story features the quiet Morgan son, whose world is rocked by feisty, sexy Karen Miller. When these familiar characters find each other, sparks fly. As always, obstacles abound, not the least of which are their vastly different personalities. Please read on for a glimpse of **Rich's Dilemma**.

Chapter 1

"We've caught it early, Rich. It's very treatable," Dr. Carina, the urologist, said. "I'm waiting for one more test, but I'm reasonably certain it will mean removal of your left testicle. That's unless we find lymph node involvement. The oncologist and I prefer to avoid chemotherapy and radiation unless absolutely necessary. We'll know better post-surgery."

Stunned, Rich Morgan stared at the short man with bushy eyebrows who bore an uncanny resemblance to Woody Allen. "When?" was all he could manage.

"The sooner the better. I'd like to schedule your pre-op for end of the week and the surgery next week. I'm at the Surgical Center on Tuesdays and Thursdays. Surgery takes about thirty to forty-five minutes. You'll need someone to drive you."

Rich sat silent, staring out the window for several minutes.

Dr. Carina placed a gentle hand on his shoulder. "You're going to be fine. The long-term prognosis for this type of cancer is good when we catch it early."

"What about kids?"

"Are you planning to have one soon?"

Rich smiled. "Not likely. There's no one in my life right now."

"This normally doesn't affect men's fertility."

"Okay, then. I guess I'm doing this. Is the recovery long? Will I need to take much time off from work?"

"I usually tell patients to take it easy for two to four weeks. No high-intensity exercise, but walking's fine. As for work, as long as it's not overly stressful or physically taxing, you should feel okay in a week or two."

Rich nodded. "Okay, let's do it."

"I'll step out and get Betsy in. She does all my scheduling." Dr. Carina left Rich alone with his thoughts. *Cancer. What will the family say? Should I even tell them? Of course I should. Hard as it is for me to take it, I'll needed their support and love.*

"Here we go," the doctor said returning with his dark-haired, middle-aged receptionist. "Betsy, what have we got next week?"

After several minutes of conversation, they set Wednesday at eight thirty in the morning for the surgery. Betsy gave him several sheets of instructions. "I'll need to call over to the Surgery Center to get you a pre-op time. Is there a good day or time for you this week?"

"Anytime's fine," he said, thanking her and folding the sheets of paper in half.

"See you next Wednesday, Rich," Dr. Carina said. "If you have any questions before then, please call me. Cell number's on the information sheet."

Mind racing, Rich exited the medical building and ran straight into Karen Miller. The armful of folders in her arms went flying, and papers scattered everywhere. "Oh gee, so sorry," he said, stooping to help her gather them.

"My fault," she said, "I was a million miles away."

Join the club, Rich thought, smiling at her despite his unsettling news. He hadn't seen her since her brother Tim's marriage to his sister Gail and thus had not acted on his fierce attraction to her. He couldn't completely explain why. Something to do with her being a spitfire and him quiet, shy, and boring. Lapis-blue eyes met his as she brushed strands of curly brown hair from her forehead. She was barely five-four, so he towered over her. "So was I. Can I help you get these back in the proper order?"

"No, I'll drop them off like this. They can sort it out."

"Do you work here?"

She flashed the radiant smile he already adored. "Nope, I work two days a week for Andy Roby the CPA."

"I didn't know you were a numbers person."

Karen laughed. "Hardly. Basically, I'm a receptionist and courier. How are you anyway? I haven't seen you since…?"

"The wedding."

"Are you okay? You look a little pale."

"Just had some unsettling news. I'm heading home to digest it. Sorry again about the collision."

"No worries. Listen, I'm just gonna drop these inside. Wanna grab a drink or even an early supper?"

Rich was about to say no, but instead said, "Sure. I'll wait out here."

*****

When Karen emerged from Cove Medical, she spied Rich Morgan sitting on a bench in the shade, looking as if he'd lost his best friend. Even in dejection, the man was gorgeous, long and lean, with that straight brown hair always falling in his face. After their collision, she'd had to fight the urge to brush it back with her fingers. Then there were his father's bushy dark eyebrows, incongruous on his otherwise perfect face. The eyebrows were sexy as hell, but they belonged on a mischievous Irishman, not the CEO of Morgan Enterprises.

"Hey, you ready?" she asked, startling him as she approached.

Rich stood, brushing hair from his brow. "I am. Where would you like to go?"

"Let's get sandwiches at the Café and walk down to your sister's garden. There are lots of shady spots there." She referred to the community garden started by his younger sister Pam that was just a short walk from the center of town.

Rich nodded. "Good idea, but she wouldn't want you calling it her garden."

Karen grinned. "I'll remember."

The Café was packed. As they made their way to the counter to order sandwiches, Rich spied two of his sisters eating with Lynn Casey, wife of Gus Casey, their farm manager. He waved but continued to follow Karen toward the takeout counter. "Hey, there's Pam and Gail," she said. "Just tell me what you want and go say hello if you want."

He didn't want, but felt awkward saying it. He handed Karen two twenty dollar bills and headed across the restaurant. "Hi, ladies," he said as he reached the table.

"Hello yourself," Gail said, grinning. "Hot date?"

"Don't start. Hi, Lynn. How are you and the kids?"

"Great."

"Dad says you guys are getting ready to build?" Morgan's Fire, their family's farm, was over five hundred acres, including several ponds, a vineyard, and prime waterfront property. When Rich's father, Richard Morgan, had lured the horse trainer east, he had written into Gus's contract the rights to a four-acre lot, location to be decided.

"Thanks to his generosity. It's a beautiful spot right on Long Pond. We're saving and planning now for next spring."

"Gonna be great to have you out there," Rich said, smiling.

Lynn looked up at him. "What about you? Think you might move out and build someday?"

"Someday. Town suits me right now."

Pam stared at her brother. "You okay?"

"Yup. Better get back to the counter," he said. "Enjoy your lunch."

As he headed to where Karen stood, Pam turned to Gail. "Did he seem off to you?"

Gail shrugged. "Hard to tell with Rich. You know he's Mr. Calm, Cool, and Collected. No emotion, no drama."

"That's just it. He didn't seem calm, cool, and collected."

Gail smiled. "Maybe he's distracted by his date with Karen?"

"Maybe," Pam said, shrugging as she turned back to their conversation.

CHAPTER 2

"How's your sandwich?" Karen asked after five minutes of sitting on the bench eating in silence.

They sat under an enormous maple at the far edge of the garden. There were few gardeners and only a couple of volunteers working at various spots. Creation of the garden the past spring had been a community effort spearheaded by Pam Morgan and supported by many. Now in midsummer, all thirty of the raised beds were bursting with bloom—flowers, vegetables, herbs, and fruit. Each gardener's style was evident in the arrangement and choice of plants.

"Can't ruin a BLT," he replied. "Especially on Josie's sourdough." He referred to Josie Connors, co-owner of the Crab Café with her husband, Paul. She was the baker, and he manned the grill. Most locals called it simply the Café, although it had been named in honor of the region's beloved horseshoe crabs.

Karen nodded, taking a bite of her chicken salad on a warm baguette. "So how do you like village life? Must seem pretty tame after living all over the world."

"I was twelve when we moved back to the States. Our life in Maine wasn't all that different from here."

"Still, you've had all those cool experiences. I've never been anywhere."

He smiled down at her, thinking she had the cutest turned-up nose he'd ever seen. "Would you like to travel?"

"Would I? Not sure how that will ever happen since I'm stuck here in Hicksville."

"You're not happy in Horseshoe Crab Cove?"

She shrugged. "It's my home. Of course I love it. It's just confining sometimes, you know?"

"Small town, big family?"

"Something like that. How about you? Is this enough for you? Do you plan to stay?"

"For now, yes. My work is here. I lived in the city after college and didn't like it much. I mean, I loved the theater and culture, but not the busyness. Everything moves so fast."

"How come a handsome guy like you isn't with someone?"

He grinned. "I had a girlfriend, but that's kind of petered out."

"Sara Gregson?"

Surprised, he said, "Yes."

"Small town, remember? Sara's a great yoga teacher."

"Yes, she is."

"So are you feeling better now?" Karen asked, her blue eyes full of concern.

He nodded, giving her a shy smile. "This was a welcome distraction. That didn't sound right, did it? I mean... I don't think of you as a distraction. It was great to run into you. I just have a lot on my mind, that's all."

"Sometimes it helps to talk about it."

Rich hesitated. A very private person, he rarely shared his thinking with anyone. It had been one of the factors in his breakup with Sara. Finally, he answered, "Kind of sucks. Excuse my language."

Karen met his eyes, saying nothing, waiting.

"I have cancer. I need surgery. Soon."

"Oh no, I'm sorry. Is it early? And treatable?"

"Yes and yes. Or at least that's what they tell me. Just a shock, you know?"

For an instant, Karen spied the fear in his beautiful hazel eyes, but just as quickly, it was gone. "Anything I can do?" she said.

"Have dinner with me sometime? Not sure if you have a boyfriend, but it could just be a friendly meal."

"Don't have a boyfriend, and I'd love to." There was something happening between them, but she couldn't quite identify it. She suppressed the urge to throw her arms around him and whisper that everything would be all right. She wondered about the cancer but didn't think she should pry further.

"Great! I mean about your willingness to have dinner. The no-boyfriend part too. Sorry, but I've got to get going. I have a meeting at the vineyard in twenty minutes."

She crumpled her sandwich wrapper and grabbed her bag. "I've got to get back to the office too."

They exchanged cell phone numbers, then walked out of the garden, waving to several of the gardeners. After going through the arbor, she pointed to the house across the street. "This is me."

"That's convenient," he said. "I didn't know you worked in the same building as Pam." His sister and another therapist, Elise Nolan, had recently moved into the renovated Victorian where they shared office and consulting space.

"Yup, but as I said, I'm only here very part-time. Our paths rarely cross."

"Enjoy the rest of your day, and I'll be in touch about dinner," he said.

Karen nodded, then stepped forward, hugging him. "I'm sure everything will be okay."

Startled, he returned her hug, wishing he could rest in her arms all day. Finally, he stepped back, "Thanks, Karen. Take care." *Whoa, she is hot, and she smells great too*, he thought, the scent of citrus and spices lingering in her wake. As he watched her walk into her building, he was aware that despite the cancer, his libido was doing just fine. *Not sure where the cancer will take me, but Karen Miller's sure something to live for!*

About the Author

M. Lee Prescott is the author of dozens of works of fiction for adults, young adults, and children, among them *Prepped to Kill, Gadfly, Lost in Spindle City,* and *Poof!* (Ricky Steele Mysteries), *A Friend of Silence, In the Name of Silence,* and *The Silence of Memory* (Roger and Bess Mysteries), *Jigsaw,* and *Song of the Spirit,* and her contemporary romance series, *Morgan's Run.* And now there is *Morgan's Fire* and book two, *Tim's Hands!* Lee is thrilled to be launching three Morgan's Fire titles in 2019. In addition to her fiction, her nonfiction books are published by Heinemann, and she has written numerous articles in the field of literacy education. Lee is a professor of education at a small New England liberal arts college, where she teaches reading and writing pedagogy. Her current research focuses on mindfulness and connections to reading and writing. She regularly teaches abroad, most recently in Singapore.

Lee has lived in southern California (loved those Laguna nights!), Chapel Hill, North Carolina, and various spots in Massachusetts and Rhode Island. Currently, she resides in Massachusetts on a beautiful river, where she canoes, swims, and watches an incredible variety of wildlife pass by. She is the mother of two grown sons and spends lots of time with them, their beautiful wives, and her beloved grandchildren. When not teaching or writing, Lee's passions revolve around family, yoga (Kripalu is a second home), swimming, sharing mindfulness with children and adults, and walking.

Lee loves to hear from readers. Email her at *mleeprescott@gmail.com*, and visit her website to hear the latest and sign up for her newsletters!

Author webpage and Newsletter sign-up:
www.mleeprescott.com

Follow me on BookBub!
www.bookbub.com/search/authors?search=M.+Lee+Prescott